# PURRFECT RIVALRY

## THE MYSTERIES OF MAX 6

### NIC SAINT

PUSS IN PRINT PUBLICATIONS

**PURRFECT RIVALRY**

**The Mysteries of Max 6**

Copyright © 2018 by Nic Saint

All rights reserved. No part of this book may be reproduced in any form by any electronic or mechanical means including photocopying, recording, or information storage and retrieval without permission in writing from the author.

This is a work of fiction. Names, characters, places, brands, media, and incidents are either the product of the author's imagination or are used fictitiously. The author acknowledges the trademarked status and trademark owners of various products referenced in this work of fiction, which have been used without permission. The publication/use of these trademarks is not authorized, associated with, or sponsored by the trademark owners.

Edited by Chereese Graves

www.nicsaint.com

Give feedback on the book at: info@nicsaint.com

facebook.com/nicsaintauthor
@nicsaintauthor

First Edition

Printed in the U.S.A

# CHAPTER 1

I woke up from a sudden chill and discovered I'd fallen asleep on the kitchen floor again. In spite of my protective layer of belly muscle insulating me against the cold, I was freezing. The first thing that occurred to me was the startling observation that the reason for my vigil—the protection of my bowl of food—had been for naught: the bowl was empty!

I quickly trotted over and gasped. To my horror, all three of my bowls had been emptied overnight: the one containing my extra-crunchy vitamin-enhanced prime-brand kibble, the one with my extra-yummy Cat Snax, and even the one with my purified fresh water, which Odelia makes sure is filled to the brim every evening before she retires to bed.

I groaned in dismay. I knew whodunit, of course. It was the whole reason I'd started my nocturnal kitchen vigil. To protect my food supply. And now my stash had been raided. Just like it had been raided the night before, and the night before and the night before that!

Gah. This was getting ridiculous.

Chilled to the bone—a condition exacerbated by the

kitchen door being ajar, another irksome habit of the food thief—I decided to warm myself in Odelia's bed. I padded out of the kitchen into the living room and then up the stairs. The sun was already making a valiant attempt to hoist itself over the horizon and would soon be casting the world in its golden hue. Time for Odelia to wake up, and for me to enjoy the best part of the day: my daily snuggle with my human, my nose pressed into her armpit while I purred up a storm and she cuddled me and made me happy to be alive.

This morning, as Odelia gently returned to the land of wakefulness, I made up my mind to have a heart-to-heart talk with her about the state of affairs at the house, and tell her straight out about my long list of grievances. She needed to get rid of the vile serpent she'd nursed at her unsuspecting bosom for far too long.

Odelia is a sweetheart. Too sweet for her own good. It was time to point a damning finger at the horrible pest who'd invaded our lives and allow things to go back to normal.

I trudged up the stairs and with some effort arrived at the top. Crossing the landing, I set paw for her room, then glanced up at the bed. Odelia sleeps in one of those boxspring contraptions, and navigating the jump onto the bed has lately proven something of a challenge. Since Odelia put me on a diet things have improved, and I now made the jump without a hitch, and more or less gracefully landed on all fours on the foot of the bed.

My human was still sleeping peacefully, her even breathing indicating she didn't have a care in the world. My heart warmed and a smile slid up my furry face. Odelia might be misguided, she's the kindest and most decent human I know, and I actually looked forward to pressing my wet and cold nose to her side and basking in the warmth of her embrace.

And I was just about to join her when I discovered to my extreme horror and dismay that a smallish orange cat had beaten me to the punch and had wriggled himself into Odelia's arms, enjoying an embrace that was rightfully mine! Diego! He'd taken my spot!

Even as I was gawking at the spectacle, my mouth opening and closing a few times in helpless fury, the foul usurper opened his eyes and gave me an insolent stare with those slate gray eyes of his, as if to say: whatcha gonna do about it, buddy?

And then he produced the most triumphant grin any cat has ever produced since cats have found it in their generous hearts to give humans the benefit of their company.

"Hey, doofus. Finally decided to wake up, huh? I thought for sure you passed out."

"I wasn't passed out. I was sleeping," I indignantly told the orange menace.

"Sure, sure. Whatever you say, bud," Diego said, and then closed his eyes again, nestling deeper into Odelia's embrace.

Her long blond tresses were spread out across the pillow, and Diego, without a doubt the foulest cat who's ever lived, eagerly dug his face into her hair, just the way I like to do, and breathed in her delicious human scent, a wicked smile spreading across his features.

"Hey," I hissed, reluctant to wake Odelia up. "That's my spot! You stole my spot!"

Diego smirked. "And now it's mine. Got a problem with that, fatso?"

My teeth came together with a click. "For your information, I'm not fat. I'm big-boned. It runs in my family. And yes, I do have a problem with that. Just like I have a problem with the fact that you ate all of my food! And that you left the door open again last night!"

"My food, you mean. And why wouldn't I eat it? Odelia put it out for me."

"It's my food and you know it! She puts out separate bowls for you and for me and you ate everything—my food *and* yours!"

"You know what, Max? I think it's time you and I laid down some ground rules. I mean, if we're going to be living together and all we need to set some boundaries."

I liked the sound of that. "Okay. First rule: don't touch my food. Second rule: don't use my litter box. Third rule: don't snuggle up to Odelia in the morning. That's my job and she hates it when other cats take over from me. I've got that extra-special snuggle she likes which, along with my extra-special purrs, puts her in a good mood for the rest of the day."

"I like your rules, Max. They seem more than fair. Which is why I'm only going to make a few slight emendations. First rule: your food is now my food. Second rule: your litter box is now my litter box. Third rule: Odelia prefers my brand of snuggles so your morning cuddle time is now my morning cuddle time." He gave me a wink. "Thanks for listening."

At this, clearly feeling he'd said what he had to say without inclination to elaborate, he closed his eyes and burrowed deeper into Odelia's armpit, purring up a storm.

To my not inconsiderate consternation, Odelia actually started stroking his fur!

Diego opened one eye as if to say, 'See? My extra-special snuggles hit the spot.'

I would have hit a spot on his head had I been less of a gentlecat. Instead, I gave Odelia a soft nudge, then, when she still refused to wake up, resorted to my trademark kneading technique: placing both front paws on her stomach and pretending it was a piece of dough that needed to be persuaded into perfect consistency and shape. And when that still didn't give me the result I was looking for, I added some claw for that extra oomph you want.

Odelia opened first one seaweed-green eye and then the other, and finally a smile spread across her features. "Max. Diego. So nice to see you guys getting along so well."

I would have lodged a formal protest had she not invited me into the crook of her right arm, even while Diego occupied the crook of her left, and soon I was purring away.

Diego might have tried to take my place in Odelia's heart, just like he'd taken my place in her home and my litter box, but it was obvious that my human still cared about me, and soon my frigid bones were warmed up again, and so was my wounded heart.

## CHAPTER 2

*H*aving woken up with not one but two cats in her arms, Odelia Poole started the new day with a smile and the distinct impression she was truly blessed.

She'd been slightly anxious when Diego entered their lives again—it's always a tough proposition for a cat to accept the introduction of a second cat into his home—but she now felt that Max was adjusting wonderfully. Soon he and Diego would be best buddies, exchanging high-fives and chasing mice together—or whatever it was that buddy cats did.

She displaced both felines, drawing a disappointed mewling sound from Max, and slid from between the covers. She placed both feet into her bunny slippers and shuffled over to the window and threw the curtains wide, allowing the sun to stream into the bedroom.

Gazing out across her modest domain—the small patch of backyard that she called her own—she reveled for a moment in the pleasant sound of birdsong and saw that a tiny sparrow was sitting in the top of a beech tree and was singing at the top of its tiny lungs.

"A private serenade," she murmured, enchanted. "Much obliged, good sir or lady."

She rubbed her eyes, then stretched and yawned cavernously. Shuffling out of her room, only half awake, she picked her way along the stairs. Before she'd imbibed a decent amount of caffeine, she usually felt as if she'd much rather still be in bed, even though her mind had decided she should kickstart her day. As the intrepid—and only—reporter for the Hampton Cove Gazette she had things to do, people to meet and articles to write.

She started the coffeemaker and rummaged around in the fridge and kitchen cupboards for something edible when she became aware of a marked chill in the air.

Searching around for the source of the cold front that had rolled in, she saw that the kitchen door was ajar. She urgently needed to install a pet door, so Max and Diego wouldn't keep pushing open the door in the middle of the night. There had been a spate of break-ins lately, and holding an open house day in and day out perhaps wasn't such a good idea.

Not that she had a lot of valuables to steal—or other stuff sneak thieves would be remotely interested in. One simply cannot amass a wealth of material possessions on a reporter's salary. But still. No sense in giving them easy access to her home and hearth.

She made a mental note to talk to her dad. Then, discovering she was out of cereal, milk and yogurt, decided not to postpone the urgent missive but deliver it in person.

So she slipped her feet into the galoshes she kept by the kitchen door, cinched her pink terry cloth robe tighter around her slight frame, and stepped out into the backyard.

Since her parents lived next door, and a convenient opening in the hedge that divided the respective backyards provided easy access, she arrived at her final destination in seven seconds flat, without breaking a sweat, cup of coffee in hand, taking occasional sips.

The hits of caffeine drove the sleep from her body, and by the time she was opening her parents' screen door and stepping into their kitchen, she was more or less human again.

"Hey, sweetie," said her mother, who was pouring herself a cup of coffee. "You're early."

"Ran out of breakfast essentials," she intimated, and started foraging the fridge. Juice, milk, yogurt... Check, check and check. She took a bowl from the cupboard over the sink, dragged down the oversized box of Corn Flakes, and started her own breakfast prep.

Her mother, who was the spitting image of Odelia, albeit with a touch of gray streaking her own blond hair, called out, "Tex, honey! Breakfast is ready!"

Taking a seat at the kitchen counter, Odelia quickly dug in, alternating between scooping up her cereal, now soaked in milk and drowned in fruit yogurt with half a banana, and sipping from her coffee, to which her mother now added creamer and a spoon of sugar.

"How are things going at the paper?" asked her mom, taking a seat at the counter.

"Great. I still have that article to finish about the new school play and the upcoming senior citizen dance—and I'm still hoping to get lucky and land that exclusive one-on-one with the one and only Charlie Dieber!"

"Ooh. Aren't you the lucky one?"

"Yeah. So far Dan struck out with Charlie's management, but I'm hoping they change their minds. Keeping my fingers crossed!"

Mom crossed her fingers and so did Odelia. They were both equally big Dieber fans.

Odelia's father, who'd entered the kitchen, asked, "Dieber. Isn't he that actor—"

"Singer, Dad."

"Right. I knew that."

Tex Poole was a large man, with a shock of white hair and an engaging smile. He was digging around the cupboards, opening door after door, until Mom said, "Food's on the table, hon."

He glanced down at the bowl of oatmeal porridge Mom had placed on the counter and grimaced. "It's at times like these that I sincerely regret attending medical school. Why couldn't I have become a plumber, and be blissfully unaware of the importance of diet?"

Mom waved a hand. "Even plumbers have to watch their cholesterol levels. No more saturated fats for you. Those levels need to come down and they need to come down before you go and have a stroke or some other horrible incident I don't even want to think about."

"Yeah, Dad," said Odelia. "Even plumbers need to look after their pipes."

"Ha ha. I never knew I raised a comedian for a daughter." He plunked down, staring at the distasteful-looking sludge, spoon raised but not making any indication to start eating it.

"Here, have some of my yogurt," Odelia said, feeling sorry for her dad, who'd been forced to put himself on a diet after discovering his cholesterol levels were off the charts.

He gratefully added some yogurt to his porridge, took a deep breath and dug in. "I know this stuff is healthy—but why does it have to taste so bad?"

"You'll get used to it," Mom said.

"Oh, Dad, if you have time, could you install a pet door over at my place?"

"I'll do it today," said her father, visibly quivering when the first spoon of oatmeal hit his esophagus and the gloop proceeded to slide down his gullet and into his stomach.

"Wasn't it today that Charlie Dieber was on Morning Sunshine?" asked Mom.

"Oh! Right! Better turn on the TV," she instructed her mother.

Mom obligingly switched on the TV set, but the story featured on the televised radio show was an item about freshly hatched chicks, and Odelia quickly lost interest.

"Looks like we just missed it," said Mom.

Just then, Odelia's grandmother waltzed into the kitchen, holding her new iPhone to her ear, and nodding seriously. "Yes, Your Holiness. But there are children dying in Angujistan every day, and we need to get a handle on the situation before things get out of hand."

Odelia exchanged a puzzled look with her mother, who merely rolled her eyes.

"Yes, Pope Francis," said Gran as she took a seat at the counter and gestured at her empty cup that read, 'Greatest Grandma in the World.' Odelia poured coffee into the cup while Gran continued her curious conversation. "Yeah, I agree we can do more, Your Holiness. Have you thought about getting in touch with the United Nations or UNICEF? I would advise you to get on the horn with Ban Ki-moon pronto, Francis. Just tell him what I just told you." Her wrinkled face creased into a wide smile. "No, *you're* welcome, Your Holiness. Us Catholics have to stick together. Yes, just doing my part for world peace."

She disconnected, placed her iPhone on the table and took a sip of coffee. Only then did she notice that the rest of her family were intently staring at her.

"What?" she asked. "Never heard a woman chat with the Pope before?"

"You were actually chatting with the pope just now?" asked Odelia. "*The* pope?"

"The one in Rome?" asked Dad, gratefully using this interruption as an excuse to put down his spoon.

Gran shook her head, causing her tiny white curls to dance around her wrinkly features. "Do you know any other popes? Of course the one in Rome. I told Francis he needs to get a handle on this Angujistan business before more people die and he agreed wholeheartedly. As he should. When a fellow Catholic calls in with an urgent message it's only natural that he would be thrilled. He told me he'd heed my most excellent advice."

"Your grandmother has been advising world leaders," said Mom at Odelia's unposed question. "She's already talked to Bong Si-moon."

"Ban Ki-moon," Gran was quick to correct her.

"That one. He runs the United Nations."

"Great guy," said Gran. "Very happy to chat."

"And who was that other one you talked to?" asked Mom.

"Try to keep up, Marge. Bill Gates. Sharp dude. We talked about providing housing for the poor. I gave him a few suggestions and he was more than happy to jot them down."

Dad gave Odelia a knowing look. "We're in the presence of greatness, Odelia."

"Yeah, forget about Charlie Dieber," Mom added. "It's your grandmother you should be interviewing."

"But how?" Odelia asked. "How do you get in touch with these people?"

Gran shrugged. "I have my ways." She hopped from the stool with surprising agility. "Gotta be going. I'm expecting a call from the President. Give him a piece of my mind."

And with these words, she stalked off, frowning at her phone and very much looking the part of the highly regarded proficient advisor to the world's political and business elite.

Odelia was going to ask her parents what the heck was going on, but Mom shushed her and turned up the volume on the TV set. As they watched, the host announced with breathless relish that shots had been fired at Charlie Dieber as he exited the studio. Visibly disappointed, the radio jockey clarified that Charlie was unharmed and that his bodyguard had sustained the brunt of the attack and had been pronounced dead at the scene.

"Sweet Jesus!" Mom cried, pressing her hands to the sides of her head. "Thank God Charlie lives!"

"Poor bodyguard, though," Odelia said, shaking her head.

"Yeah, imagine having to take a bullet for Charlie Dieber," Dad quipped.

Mom shut him up with a pointed look. "The man died so Charlie could live. He's a hero and a saint and should be praised for his brave and selfless act."

Dang. Mom was an even bigger Bedieber than Odelia would have guessed.

She promptly got up. "This is big," she announced. "I have to get over there and break this story."

"And while you're at it don't forget to ask for Charlie's autograph, honey," Mom said as she moved to the door.

"If I get within ten feet of Charlie I'm not going to nag him about autographs, Mom."

"You promised!" she called out after her.

"That was before someone tried to drill a hole in him!"

# CHAPTER 3

We were seated in Odelia's backyard, me, Dooley and Brutus, for an emergency meeting. Hidden behind the gardenias, from time to time ducking our heads up to see if the coast was clear and we weren't being overheard, we conducted our meeting with the stealth and solemnity the situation demanded. We were at war, and it was all paws on deck.

"He ate all your food?" asked Dooley. The gray Ragamuffin looked shocked.

"Everything. Every last morsel," I confirmed.

"That's not very nice."

"Not nice?! It's downright criminal!"

"You can have some of my food," Dooley magnanimously offered. "There's plenty."

"Yeah, have some of mine, too," said Brutus, a powerfully built black cat who'd been my mortal enemy until not all that long ago. In fact the arrival of Diego had created a bond between us that had wiped out our former enmity and turned us into unlikely allies instead.

"Will you look at that?" Dooley asked, a somber note in his voice.

We peeked through the gardenias and Brutus drew in a sharp breath when he saw Diego seated on the terrace with Harriet, pressing their paws together in a cloying picture of loved-up cuteness. Any moment Celine Dion could burst into the *Titanic* theme song.

"Don't look, Brutus. Just don't look," I advised the cat, who'd been Harriet's beau before Diego's fateful return.

But Brutus couldn't tear his eyes away from the train wreck even if he wanted to. Nor could I, actually, or Dooley, who'd also been one of Harriet's admirers. In fact it was safe to say I was probably the only male feline for miles around who'd never been into the white Persian. No idea why that was. Probably the fact that she was one of those haughty specimens, who enjoyed lording it over other cats, a quality that set my teeth on edge.

"This is too much," growled Brutus. "Stealing your food. Stealing my girlfriend—"

"Stealing my litter box and my morning cuddle with Odelia," I said somberly.

They gawked at me. "He uses your litter box?" asked Brutus. "Say it isn't so, Max!"

I nodded in confirmation. "Sadly, yes. I've been forced to do my business in Odelia's rhododendrons ever since Diego's return. No way am I going to suffer the indignation of relieving myself in a place that reeks of Diego. Talk about suffering the ultimate humiliation."

Brutus and Dooley sat in stunned silence, as they imagined having to share a litter box with Diego. This was bad, their silence seemed to indicate. This was extremely bad.

"Did you say he stole your morning cuddle with Odelia?" asked Dooley.

"He did." I proceeded to describe my shock and dismay

when I discovered Diego snuggling up to Odelia that morning. How he didn't even bat an eye when I confronted him.

"Oh, the horror," muttered Brutus. "The heartbreak. The infuriating gall of the cat!"

"We have to do something about this, you guys," I said. "I feel like he's slowly but surely trying to get rid of me. Before I know it, Odelia will vote Diego Most Valuable Cat."

"Odelia would never do that," said Dooley, eyes wide. "Would she?"

"I wouldn't be surprised if Diego is trying to poison Odelia's mind," said Brutus.

I stared at him. "Poison Odelia? But why?"

"Poison her mind—set her against you."

"No way," Dooley gasped. "There's just no way!"

"Oh, yes, there is," Brutus assured him. "He'll feed her all kinds of lies. Start with something innocuous, like the fact that Max left some poop on the floor, for instance."

Dooley turned to me. "Max! Did you poop on the floor?"

"Of course I didn't poop on the floor! He's talking about Diego."

"Diego pooped on the floor?!"

"Oh, Dooley," I said. "Try to pay attention."

"*Diego* could poop on the floor," Brutus explained, "and then tell Odelia *Max* did it."

The pure deviousness of the scheme seemed to shock Dooley, for he audibly gasped.

"And when she's finally had enough, she'll get rid of Max," Brutus continued.

"Get rid of me!"

Brutus nodded somberly. "The animal shelter, Max. Where all cats go to die."

"Noooo!"

"Oh, yes. Mark my words. Before you know it, you'll be locked up in a cage the size of a shoebox, waiting to be gassed or whatever it is that they do at these establishments."

I sank back on my haunches, the terrible fate that awaited me suddenly looming large and ominous. "I don't want to go to the shelter, you guys. I don't want to be gassed!"

"You might get an injection," Brutus said. "I've heard some even offer electrocution."

His words provided no comfort. I'd suffered injections from Vena Aleman, Odelia's go-to veterinarian. And I'd seen *The Green Mile.* No electrocution for me, thank you very much.

"We have to stop him," I said, a tremor in my voice. "We have to do something."

"Before Diego poops on the floor," Dooley added, his mind stuck on that image.

"Then let's get rid of this pest," said Brutus, pointing a resolute claw at Diego.

"But how? We tried to get rid of him before, remember? He's hard to dislodge."

"There's only one cat in this town who's ever managed to get rid of Diego," said Brutus, "and that's Clarice. We have to find her and convince her to repeat the procedure."

"I remember," I said, cheering up a little. Clarice is a feral cat, Hampton Cove's very own dumpster-diving feline superhero, swatting away lesser cats with a flick of her paw and putting the fear of God into everyone she meets. Even though I'm scared stiff of her—and so are Dooley and Brutus—she's helped us out on more than one occasion, and even received a standing invitation from Odelia to raid her supply of cat food any time she wants. Not that she ever shows her whiskers around here. She prefers to traipse through the woods that surround our small hamlet, roaming around unfettered like the maverick cat that she is.

"Brutus is right, Max," said Dooley. "Clarice is our only hope."

"I don't know," I said. "Last time she drove him away he quickly returned. What's to make him stay away now? And who's to say Clarice will want to do our dirty work for us?"

"Max is right, Brutus," said Dooley. "Clarice takes orders from no one."

"We're not going to order her around," said Brutus. "We'll ask her nicely. In exchange for a lifetime supply of Cat Snax I'm sure even she can be persuaded to do the right thing."

"Brutus is right, Max," said Dooley. "No one says no to a lifetime supply of Cat Snax."

"Clarice is going to need more than Cat Snax. You guys, we're talking about a cat who feeds on mice and rats and who knows what else. This is a raw foodie—not a pampered pet."

"Max is right—"

"Oh, shut up, Dooley," Brutus growled. "So we'll offer her raw meat—I don't care. If I have to I'll catch her some nasty, hairy rats myself. *Anything* to get rid of that horrible pest." He turned a vicious eye on Diego, who was now exchanging tender smooches with Harriet, and lowered his voice to a menacing snarl. "That cat's got to go, before I commit felinicide."

CHAPTER 4

Odelia parked her dinged-up pickup around the corner from the radio station and got out. Hiking her purse higher up her shoulder and smoothing her purple blouse and jeans skirt, she set foot for the place where the terrible events had unfolded. Chase Kingsley's pickup stood parked haphazardly across the curb, and so did her uncle Alec's cruiser. And as she drew closer to the W-AWOL5 radio station, she saw that a small mass of onlookers stood rubbernecking while Hampton Cove's finest were going about their business of finding clues.

There wasn't all that much to see, actually, as the Dieber himself and his crew were long gone—no doubt ducking into a limo and racing from the scene with screaming tires the moment the shots rang out—but young girls with Dieber T-shirts and Dieber banners still stood lining the sidewalk, just the way they'd done when their idol was exiting the station.

W-AWOL5 was housed on the first floor of a nondescript building, a temp agency occupying the ground floor. And as Odelia approached she saw that police officers working for Uncle Alec were busy talking to the hordes of Dieber fans and other witnesses, no doubt extracting statements from each and every one of them.

And that's when she caught sight of her uncle himself, standing out because of his sizable bulk—her uncle was easily thrice as big as she was—and his snazzy Chief of Police uniform. He stood scratching his ruddy face and russet sideburns, looking decidedly puzzled.

"Hey, Uncle Alec," she said as she joined him on the curb.

"Odelia, honey," he said by way of greeting, then slapped a hand to his brow. "I should have called you. Totally forgot." He shook his head. "It's been a real shit storm."

"I can only imagine. Is this where it happened?" She was pointing at a spot on the pavement, which was marked with a chalk outline of a body.

"Yeah. That's where he dropped dead. Name of Ray Cooper. Only been a bodyguard for a year or so. Played pro ball before—Green Bay Packers. After he retired from the game he decided to go into the personal protection racket, and ended up on Dieber's security detail. Can you imagine taking a bullet for that annoying little twerp? Talk about bad luck."

Odelia grinned. "Not a big fan, are you, Uncle Alec?"

"Nope. Can't stand the kid. I mean, if you're going to take a bullet, do it for the President, or a talented dude like Bruce Springsteen or Garth Brooks. Not some obnoxious tattoo junkie who can't sing for crap and has the mentality of a spoiled brat."

"Talking about the Dieber, I presume?" asked Chase, walking up.

Odelia smiled up at the tall cop—who also happened to be her boyfriend. "Hey, Chase. So are you a Bedieber?"

"I'm with Alec on this one," the lanky detective intimated, his blue eyes flashing with good humor and his lips curling into a slight grin. "If you're going to take a bullet for someone, better have that someone be more of a mensch and less of a pain in the neck."

"Well, I'm a fan," she said. "I think he's got a great voice, and I love all of his songs."

Both men groaned. "I guess there's no accounting for taste," said Alec.

It was obvious they were going to have to agree to disagree on this one.

"So what happened, exactly?" she asked, deciding to change the subject.

"Well, Dieber and his entourage left the radio station," said Uncle Alec, gesturing at the entrance that was located right next to the temp agency. "Hundreds of fans waiting when he walked out—his team had anticipated the warm reception so they had bodyguards in a diamond formation escorting the star to a waiting limo while others assisted some of our guys with crowd control, keeping the fans behind the barriers the town council had us erect. And that's when someone decided to take a shot at Dieber but hit Ray Cooper instead."

"Did they miss? Or did Cooper throw himself in front of the shot?"

"That's what we're trying to determine," said Chase, his smile vanishing. "So far Dieber's people haven't exactly been obliging. In fact I'm going over there later. Try to get them to cooperate. Wanna join me?"

She jumped at the chance. "Talk to the Dieber? Are you kidding? Of course!"

"Cool it, Bedieber. This is a murder investigation, not a meet and greet."

"I know that," she said, trying to inject a modicum of solemnity into her demeanor. Her radiant smile gave her away, though. So far Dan's attempts to land her an exclusive sit-down had been a bust. Now she would get some face time with the star after all. Though instead of asking him about his love life she'd have to confine herself to threats made against his life.

She didn't care. She was going to meet her biggest idol—yay! She just hoped she'd be able to restrain herself, and not go all fangirl on him. Though she was sure Chase's presence would keep her feet on the ground and prevent her from making a complete fool of herself.

"I'm heading back to the station," Alec announced. "Not much more we can do here."

Odelia decided to tag along. If she was going to get to the bottom of this she needed to stick to Chase and her uncle like glue. The funny thing was, they usually let her. Even though she was a reporter she had great instincts as a snoop, and had helped them out on more than one case.

"You know?" said Chase as they walked back to their respective vehicles. "Your status as an official Bedieber just might come in handy. You know an awful lot about the guy, huh?"

"Ask me anything," she said.

"How does a kid who sounds like a sickly goat become a global pop sensation?" asked Alec.

"Ask me anything not insulting," she amended.

"Why don't you join us on the investigation?" Chase suggested. "I have a feeling this might prove a tough one to break, and if Dieber meets a true groupie like you, he just might be more accommodating to our line of questioning. Open up, if you know what I mean."

She frowned, not knowing whether to be insulted or complimented. "For your information, I'm not a groupie. I'm just a very big fan. I think he's extremely talented."

"Exactly. The guy obviously has a gigantic ego—all those big stars do—and if I take you along to stroke it…" He spread his arms. "Done deal, babe."

She shook her head as she hopped into her pickup. "You know what? If I didn't know any better I'd say you were jealous, Kingsley."

"Jealous! What's there to be jealous about?"

"His success? His mega-fortune? His millions of fans?"

He made a throwaway gesture with his hand as he, too, climbed into his pickup. "I'm not jealous. Of that knucklehead? Puh-lease."

She shared a quick smile with her uncle, who was shaking his head at their war of words. "Kids—do try to get along, will you? We've got a murder to solve, and a killer to catch. Preferably before he kills Odelia's personal hero."

His words startled her. And as she started up her car, she realized he was right.

Someone was trying to kill Charlie Dieber. And if they didn't catch this guy before he succeeded, those millions of Bediebers—not to mention Mom—would be devastated.

## CHAPTER 5

Odelia slipped her pickup into a free parking spot in front of the police station and climbed out, slamming the door shut. A big chunk of rust dropped down. She ignored it. When you drive a car as aged as hers, this kind of thing was to be expected.

Inside the station house she was greeted by sheer pandemonium. Usually not much happened in Hampton Cove—from time to time a flurry of activity would keep its police force engaged, but pretty soon things would return to normal. Now, however, the town's finest were locked into a feverish attempt to nail the perp who'd taken a shot at Dieber and missed.

Officers moved in and out of offices and interview rooms, and everywhere she looked teens and preteens occupied the space otherwise reserved for the town drunks, hard-partying weekend tourists and the elderly, complaining about those same hard-partying weekend tourists and those selfsame drunks using their mailboxes to relieve themselves.

She walked through to her uncle's office at the end of a long corridor and gave the doorjamb a knock on her way in.

The big guy was looking more than a little unnerved, the few hairs on his head that had survived attrition in disarray and his facial expression frazzled.

"You gotta help us out here, honey," he told her, rifling through his desk.

"Sure. What do you need?"

"Chase is heading into interview room number one to talk to one of the witnesses. Can you give him a hand? We need to get through all of them but we don't want to keep them too long either, or else their moms and dads will get all worked up and give us hell."

"How many have you got?"

"Heck if I know. Dozens, probably. That Dieber kid sure knows how to attract a crowd."

"Yeah, for a singer who can't sing he sure is popular, isn't he?" she said with a grin.

He leveled a comical look at her from beneath bushy brows, then continued rifling through his desk.

"What are you looking for?"

"My glasses!" he cried, throwing up his hands. "I know I left them in here somewhere before I got called out to the radio station and now I can't find the damned things! How the hell am I supposed to organize a bunch of interviews if I can't even read my own notes?!"

She pointed at his head, where his glasses were perched. His eyes rolled up, then he placed his hands on his head, retrieved the glasses without a hitch, and put them on his nose with a grateful nod in her direction. "Thanks, honey. I'm a doofus and you're a lifesaver."

"Oh, Uncle Alec," she said before leaving the office, "I asked Dad to install a pet door at my place. Could you give him a hand? Before he goes and destroys the house, I mean?"

Uncle Alec nodded. "I'll see what I can do. And if you and

Chase catch me this killer before he takes another shot at Dieber, I might even get to it sooner rather than later."

She stepped out of her uncle's office, leaving him to coordinate the investigation, and headed over to interview room number one, where Chase was already talking to a particularly nervous-looking girl who couldn't have been older than fourteen. She was accompanied by her mother, who looked as uncomfortable being there as her daughter.

They all looked up when she walked in, and she gave them a smile that she hoped would put them at ease. "Hey there," she said. "My name is Odelia Poole and I'll be assisting Detective Kingsley with the interview if that's all right with you guys."

She darted a quick look at Chase, who gave her a curt nod.

"Miss Poole is a civilian consultant," he explained. "She helps us out from time to time. Now what can you tell us about what happened this morning, Kayla? In your own time, and in your own words, please."

Kayla's mother turned to her daughter. "Just tell them what you saw so we can get out of here, honey."

The girl looked like a deer in the headlights, her eyes swiveling from Chase to Odelia and back to her mother. "I saw Charlie. He was coming out of the building. We'd been waiting for what felt like hours—me and Janet. And my mom, of course," she added softly, as if embarrassed that her mother would have been there, too.

"Who's Janet?" asked Odelia. "Is she your friend?"

Kayla nodded. She was of slight build, with long dark hair and large brown eyes that now were wide and terrified. She was wringing her hands, and Odelia saw she had a temporary tattoo of a kitten on her wrist—a Bedieber thing. At least she hoped it was a temporary tattoo and not a permanent one, as she seemed kinda young to start inking up.

"Janet and I are Charlie's biggest fans."

"That's an understatement," said her mother, settling back in her chair. She was a large woman, with a perpetual frown that had cut a deep groove between her brows. It made her look annoyed and put out, even though she didn't appear to be particularly unfriendly. Merely concerned, which was understandable under the circumstances.

"When we heard Charlie was coming to town, I thought I'd die," said Kayla. "We just had to see him. I barely slept last night, and we were out at the radio station three hours before he arrived."

"I had to put my clock at five," the mother explained. "And she still beat me to the bathroom. We arrived at six, and the fans were already three rows thick. Unbelievable."

"Better *bediebe* it," Chase said with a smile, in an attempt to break the ice. The mother merely gave him another one of her dark scowls and Chase's smile disappeared.

"So we saw Charlie arrive—in a white limo and surrounded by his bodyguards," Kayla continued, scratching at her tattoo. "He waved at us, but he didn't stop, like I'd hoped."

"The least he could have done was sign a few autographs," said her mother. "But no, he went straight from his limo to W-AWOL5 without breaking stride. Barely looked our way."

"He had to be live on the air at nine, Mom," said Kayla, defending her idol. "He didn't have time to say hi. I'm sure that he'd planned to talk to us later, after his interview."

"Yeah, and look how that worked out."

"What happened when he came out of the building, Kayla?" asked Odelia gently.

The teen swallowed at the memory. "We all yelled for him to come over and say hi."

"I yelled the loudest," said her mother. "Not because I'm

such a big fan of the dude, but my dogs were killing me and I was desperate to get out of there."

"Your dogs?" asked Chase.

"My feet, detective. I had sore feet, okay?"

"I'm pretty sure he was going to come over and talk to us," Kayla continued, "but then suddenly there was this loud bang, like an explosion, and when I looked over, Charlie was on the ground, his sunglasses all askew, and his bodyguards were all over him."

"The kid looked scared shitless," commented the mother.

"No, he didn't," Kayla said. "He was just worried about being shot."

"Well, someone did just try to kill him," Chase said.

"And then his bodyguards sort of shoved him into the limo and they drove off with tires squealing," Kayla finished her story. "It all happened so fast I didn't even know what was going on until later, when Janet told me someone had just tried to kill Charlie. If I'd known—"

"You wouldn't have done a thing," her mother said. "I wouldn't have let you."

Kayla gave her mother a defiant look. "I would have thrown myself in front of Charlie, Mom, and so would Janet. We would have saved him, just like that hero bodyguard did."

The mother shook her head, as if to say, 'Kids.'

"Did you see who shot the bodyguard, Kayla?" asked Odelia.

"No, I didn't. Like I said, it all happened real quick. And I was focused on Charlie. He looked so fine—just like in the pictures and on YouTube, only better, because he was really there. Like, for real and all." She then gave Odelia a hopeful look. "I heard he's staying in town—to prepare for his world tour. Do you know where he's staying?"

"Um, I think at some compound near the beach?" said

Odelia. "Though I'm sure he'll be heavily guarded. Especially after what happened this morning."

Kayla nodded, and Odelia could tell she was already making plans to stake out Charlie's mansion, along with her friend Janet, hoping to catch another glimpse of the singer, and this time maybe even get her hands on that coveted autograph.

"Is there anything else you want to know?" asked Kayla's mother, placing a protective arm around her daughter's shoulder. "If not, I'd like to get out of here. I need to go to work, and Kayla needs to go to school."

Kayla looked dismayed at the prospect. "Mom! I can't go to school. Not after what happened. It's like going back to school after-after-after President Kennedy was shot!"

"Trust me, honey, Charlie Dieber is no Kennedy. And besides, he's not dead, is he?"

"But—"

"No buts. You already missed half a day of classes—I don't want you to miss the rest, too. You're going to school and you're going to forget all about this terrible business. And so am I," she added, her frown deepening as she spoke.

Outside the interview room, Chase and Odelia watched as Kayla and her mother walked away, still arguing about going to school or not. It was obvious that now that she'd been through such a life-changing event, the girl wasn't ready to sit in school and learn about geography or math. She wanted to hang out at Charlie's place with her friend instead.

"And?" asked Chase. "What do you think?"

"I'm thinking that these girls make lousy witnesses. They were all so focused on Charlie that they didn't see anything else."

"And I think you're right," said Chase, dragging his fingers through his curly brown hair. "But we're still going to have to go through each and every witness report in hopes of finding something we can use."

Just then, Uncle Alec walked up. "We're collecting all the video and picture material from everyone who was outside that radio station. Can you start combing through it? I have to warn you though—it's a lot. Looks like every single person waiting for the Dieber to come out had his or her smartphone up and was filming the whole thing." He nodded at his niece. "Which is a good thing. We might get lucky, and nail this guy before he tries again."

Chase and Odelia moved into one of the larger rooms near the back of the police station, where a technician had set up a computer and was busy downloading data from the dozens of phones and other devices confiscated from the witnesses being interviewed.

They both took a seat behind the computer and the techie showed them how to access the data. For the next two hours Odelia saw more footage of Charlie Dieber than she'd ever seen before. Unfortunately it was all the same scene, and at no point did the famous singer break out into song, or show them some of his smooth dance moves. All he did was bite the dust over and over again, looking like a kid who'd just crapped his pants.

Chase seemed to enjoy the look of pure terror on the singer's face—Odelia did not.

"I think this must be his best performance yet," Chase commented after they'd gone through the scene about a dozen times, each time shot from a different angle. "I wouldn't be surprised if this got him the Oscar for best performance in a comedy."

"Ha ha. Very funny, Chase. How would you react if someone tried to shoot you?"

"I'd definitely not look like that."

"Like what?"

"Like a bunny rabbit about to be put down by the big, bad hunter."

"I think you're prejudiced. So maybe you should recuse yourself from this case."

"Like hell I should. I'm not prejudiced. I just don't care about the kid is all."

"Which is exactly why you shouldn't be on this case. Only someone who truly cares about Charlie Dieber will do their level best to bring his shooter to justice."

"You mean someone like you."

"That's right."

"Honey, if I can't be on this case because I don't like Charlie Dieber, neither can half the cops in this outfit. Mostly because we're not thirteen-year-old girls with braces."

"I'm not a thirteen-year-old girl," she said defensively. "And I got rid of my braces a long time ago."

He gave her a grin. "I would have loved to see you in braces. I'll bet you looked cute as a button."

"I think I still have them somewhere," she said, her belly going slightly weak at his wolfish grin.

"Don't tempt me. We still have a couple more hours of this stuff to go through."

And so they had. Not that any of it was in any way helpful. None of the footage showed anything beyond Charlie hitting the deck, and being bundled into his stretch limo.

# CHAPTER 6

We'd been scoping out the back alleys of Hampton Cove for what felt like hours—looking for Clarice in what I knew to be her usual haunts and hangouts. For some reason Clarice likes dumpsters. No idea why. I find them foul places where only death and decay lurk. Not to mention the odor they spread is positively foul. But to each their own, I guess, and since Clarice likes dumpsters, that's where we had to be if we wanted to find her.

"I'm tired, Max," said Dooley after we'd tapped yet another dumpster and called out Clarice's name in the faint hope of getting a response. "Maybe we can do this some other time?"

"We can't do this some other time," I told him. "Have you forgotten what's at stake?"

He gave me a blank look, so I decided to remind him.

"If we don't dislodge Diego from my home he's going to extend me the same courtesy."

He stared at me, clearly not comprehending.

"If we don't kick him out, he's going to kick me out!"

"Oh—right. Of course. Only, he won't do that, will he? He may be bad, but he's not bad to the bone."

"He is, Dooley," I assured my friend. "That cat *is* bad to the bone."

"Can you guys shut up already and give me a paw?" Brutus called out from the back of the alley. He'd been going from dumpster to dumpster, giving each one a hard rattle, calling out Clarice's name all the while.

"I don't think we'll find Clarice, Max," Dooley said, now really deciding to embrace his inner voice of gloom. "Remember she likes to hang out in the woods near the Writer's Lodge? I'm sure she's out there right now, being fed by some writer with writer's block."

Dooley was right. The first time we ever met Clarice was out in the woods, near Hetta Fried's place. Hetta rents out a small cabin to writers and other creative desperados, eager to escape their busy lives and hone their craft surrounded by all of nature and woodland creatures like Clarice. And since these creative geniuses usually are the top of the cream and have money to burn, they treat their temporary feline companions very well indeed.

"Maybe you're right," I said. "Maybe we should expand our search to the lodge."

"Of course I'm right. I'll bet she's curled up on the lap of Stephen King or Dan Brown or JK Rowling, being fed Cat Snax. She might even feature in one of their next books."

"Wouldn't that be great?" I asked, licking my paw and making a face when I realized I'd stepped into a piece of rotten fish.

"Wouldn't what be great, Max?"

"To be the cat of a famous writer, and feature in their books?"

"And when they turn that book into a movie, to be asked

to star as yourself in the Hollywood version," Dooley said excitedly.

"I think I'd want to be in a Dan Brown book," I said. "To be Professor Langdon's feline sidekick. And then I could be in the movie with Tom Hanks."

"I'd want to be in the sequel to the Hunger Games. Fight the forces of evil side by side with Jennifer Lawrence," said Dooley, a dreamy look coming over his face.

"Or to be in a new Harry Potter movie!" I cried. "To be a shapeshifting cat, capable of amazing feats of witchcraft. And a chance to hang out with Emma Watson, of course."

We both sat gazing into the middle distance for a moment, the roseate glow of our Hollywood careers lending me a momentary respite from the stark reality of my life.

"You know? Maybe this isn't such a bad idea," Dooley suddenly said. "I mean, since Odelia is going to kick you out and all, you're going to want to find a new home anyway, Max. You could do worse than Tom Hanks or Emma Watson."

I gave him my best scowl. "I'm not going to be kicked out, Dooley. Not if I can help it."

"No, but I mean, Tom or Emma might adopt you after the shoot is over. But you're going to have to work hard to ingratiate yourself. Really put in the time to win them over."

I turned my back on him. This was not what I wanted to hear.

"You'll have to show them Lovable Max, Max. Not Grumpy Max!" he called out.

"Oh, go away, Dooley," I said, thumping my paw against a dumpster.

"That is not the way to make friends and influence people, Max."

I snarled something under my breath. Dooley was right,

though. If we didn't find Clarice soon, I was doomed. Doomed to roam these back alleys and fend for myself and snack on rotten fish until I blew out my final breath. Not an agreeable prospect.

"Give us a smile, Max!" Dooley was shouting. "Show us those snappers!"

In response, I thumped the next dumpster extra hard, hoping against hope that Clarice would suddenly materialize, just like she had those previous times, and help us out.

"I don't think she's here, buddy," said Brutus when I'd reached the end of the alley.

"She's probably hanging out at the Writer's Lodge," I told him, and explained about Clarice's habit to keep aspiring and accomplished artists alike company out at the Lodge.

"That's a pretty long hike, Max," he said. "I mean—I don't mind going out there, but it's going to take us the better part of the day."

I was touched by this sudden display of selflessness on the part of my former nemesis. "You would do that for me, Brutus? Go all the way out to the woods to find Clarice?"

He frowned. "I'm not doing this for you, Max. I'm doing this for me. Or have you forgotten that Diego is moving in on my girl? If I don't get that cat out of the picture, Harriet will never take me back. For some reason that cat's got the fatal attraction thing nailed."

"I think the fatal attraction thing involves a bunny," said Dooley, who'd joined us.

I gave Brutus a cold stare. "And here I thought you were my friend," I said.

"I *am* your friend," said Brutus. "I mean, I hated your guts before. Always thought you were too hoity-toity for my taste. But now that I've come to know you I've got to admit you're a great cat to hang out with. But you're not the only one with Diego issues, Max."

"I don't have Diego issues," said Dooley. "But I want him gone anyway. Cause I don't want Max to be kicked out of Odelia's house." He placed a paw on my shoulder. "You're my friend, too, Max, and I don't want you to go and live with Emma Watson or Tom Hanks."

"Thanks, Dooley," I said, my voice breaking a little. "And you, Brutus. This means a lot to me, you guys. It's so great to have real friends who've got my back."

"We're in this together," Brutus said earnestly. "And together is how we will succeed."

Suddenly, the sound of applause startled us, and when we looked up we saw that none other than Diego was seated on the wall that dead-ended the alley, and was clapping his paws. The sound was muffled, for cat paws have cushions, which makes it hard for us to clap. Still, Diego managed just fine, and I could see his lips pucker into his customary sneer.

"I'm touched," he said. "So much love and affection. It's almost as if the seventies are back. Next you'll want to be wearing flowers in your hair and talk about brotherly love."

"What do you want?" Brutus growled, his face taking on a menacing scowl.

"Want? From you losers? Nothing. You provide me with a lot of entertainment, though. In fact you idiots are more fun to watch than *The Big Bang Theory*. For my money, Max is Leonard, Brutus is Howard, and Dooley is Raj. That only leaves Sheldon, but I think we can all agree that he's too smart for a bunch of morons like yourselves."

"And what about Penny?" asked Dooley, who seemed interested in this comparison.

"Great question, *Raj*," said Diego musingly. "I'd like to say that Harriet is Penny, and I'm the one she's decided to give her heart to."

"So... who are you?" asked Dooley, a look of confusion stealing over his features.

"I'm the cat who's canceling the show and launching his own spinoff."

"Like… The Big Diego Theory?"

"I like that," Diego admitted with an indulgent smirk. "Though I might go with The Diego and Harriet Show. Cause it's gonna be Diego and Harriet doing the horizontal mambo every hour, on the hour."

"Don't even think about it," grunted Brutus. "Your little show won't even make it past the writing stage. The network will cancel you before you make it into production."

"Me and Odelia, who's the network executive in charge of greenlighting new shows, are this close," he said, holding his claws an inch apart, "and she told me my show's a go."

I was having a hard time following the analogy, but I didn't like what I was hearing. "Odelia told you… what, exactly?"

He shrugged. "Odelia is tired of you, Max. Oh, she liked you well enough in the beginning, but after seeing your ugly mug moping around the house all these years she's in the market for something new. Something fresh and exciting." He gestured at himself. "*Moi.*"

"I don't believe you," I said. "Odelia would never say something like that."

"She would never say it to your face, Max, which is why she said it to me. She's had it with you. She's sick and tired of having some fat slob stalking her and she's thinking hard about how to get rid of you so you'll never come back."

"She-she told you this?"

"Sure she did. And don't even think about asking her about it. She'll deny everything, of course."

"He's lying, Max," said Brutus. "He's full of crap. Just like he's full of crap about the Diego and Harriet Show. Harriet would never star in a show with the likes of you, Diego. Harriet loves me."

Diego laughed. "It would be funny if it wasn't so sad." He gave us a horrendously fake pout. "Poor Brutus. Dumped by his sweetheart. And soon dumped by his human, too."

"My human would never dump me. Chase is crazy about me."

"No, he's not. And neither are Marge or Vesta. Or Tex for that matter. The Pooles are done with you three—yeah, you, too, Dooley. Out with the old—in with the new." He shook his head and tsk-tsked. "If I were you, I'd do the honorable thing and leave now, with your dignity intact. Beats being kicked out and humiliated by the Pooles. Oh, and you don't have to thank me for the heads-up. I believe in doing the right thing. That's the kind of cat I am."

"I'm going to get you for this," Brutus said, holding up one paw, his claws extending menacingly.

"Wow, Wolverine!" said Diego, laughing. "You and whose army?"

"Clarice," said Dooley. "She's going to help us get rid of you."

"Dooley, shut up!" I hissed. "She's our secret weapon—emphasis on *secret*."

"Clarice is gone," said Diego, casually giving his paw a lick.

"Gone?" I asked, and I could see the consternation on Brutus and Dooley's faces.

"How can she be gone?" asked Dooley.

"He's lying," said Brutus. "Can't you see he's lying through his teeth?"

"Oh, no, I'm not," said Diego, then fixed us with a nasty stare. "Why do you think I came back? I took care of Clarice. Payback for what she did to me. She's gone, dudes. And she's never coming back. I made sure of that." And then he produced the most hideous laugh I'd ever heard. It chilled me to the bone. When I glanced up again—Poof!—he was gone.

Vaguely, I registered Dooley yelping and crying, "He vanished in a puff of smoke! He's a demon!" I was too stunned to respond. Had Diego killed Clarice? It wasn't possible. Or was it?

CHAPTER 7

Odelia rubbed her eyes. Staring at footage of Dieber dropping to the ground was not her idea of a fun time. When Chase chuckled, she opened her eyes again. "What's so funny?"

"You! The Dieber fan can't even watch a few hours of her idol without nodding off."

"I can watch a few hours of Dieber singing—not the same footage over and over again of him dropping down on his patootie." Though she had to admit he had a fine patootie. Not as fine as Chase's, but definitely up there on the Billboard Patootie Top 100.

"I wonder," said Chase musingly.

"Wonder what?"

"If he's got a tattoo on his patootie, too. I mean, he's got tattoos on every other body part, right?"

"I wouldn't know," she said dismissively. She wasn't going to discuss Charlie's tattoos with a non-fan.

"I'll bet you do. I'll bet you know every single tattoo the kid's ever gotten, and you even know their exact significance."

"And what if I do? What's it to you?"

"Do you have tats?"

She cleared her throat and pointed at the screen. "Oh, look. Is that the killer?"

Chase laughed. "So you do. Where is it and can I see it?"

She rolled her eyes, then reluctantly got up, turned around and lifted her blouse, displaying a small tattoo on her lower back. It was a butterfly, drawn in blue and pink pastel.

"I like it," he said finally, gently rubbing his finger along the butterfly. The touch of his hand sent shivers tickling up her spine, followed by a rush of heat, and suddenly she wished he'd put his hands on some of her other body parts. The ones that weren't tattooed.

She quickly dropped her blouse before things got out of hand. There are places where getting out of hand is fine. Like her living room couch. Hampton Cove police station? No way.

"When did you get it?"

"When I was in college. A friend of mine was into tats, and she convinced me to try one. I have to admit I wasn't entirely sober when I made the decision, but very happy that my lapse of judgment didn't get me into greater trouble. And very grateful that that particular tattoo shop had a policy in place not to tattoo on visible places on the body like necks or hands or—gasp—the face."

"Yeah, imagine having that butterfly tattooed on your forehead."

"And what if I had?" she challenged.

He smiled. "I guess I'd have to get a matching one of my own."

She was touched. "Aww. You'd do that for me?"

"I'd do that for me. Who doesn't want a tattoo of a bug on their face?"

She slapped him on the shoulder, but then noticed something odd on the screen and frowned. "Isn't that the guy who was shot?"

They watched as the shot rang out and Ray Cooper scrunched up his face. The burly protection agent stumbled backwards, knocking into one of his colleagues, before crumpling into a heap, desperately clutching at his chest.

"Finally," said Chase. "Some footage of the actual shooting."

They watched the video again, but as far as Odelia could see there was no trace of the gunman. "Was he shot at close range?"

"They're still looking into that, but yeah, I think he was shot at fairly close range."

"So the gunman should be in this clip."

They watched the same footage a few more times, but if the gunman was in it, they couldn't find him. At least they now had the incident on film. "I'll send this to forensics," said Chase. "Maybe they can see things we can't. Enhance certain parts or apply some of that CSI mumbo-jumbo to establish a time frame and a blow-by-blow of what happened, exactly."

Odelia nodded. She hoped he was right. With the kind of high-tech stuff that was available these days, maybe they could unearth things that were invisible at first glance.

There was a knock at the door, and Uncle Alec walked in, followed by a stern-faced man in a three-piece suit that looked like it might have cost a thousand bucks. A lawyer, she knew before Alec introduced the guy.

"This is Paul Seymour," said the Chief. "Counselor Seymour works for Charlie Dieber. Detective Chase Kingsley, who's in charge of the case. And Odelia Poole, civilian consultant."

"Detective. Miss Poole," said the lawyer. "I only have one question for you at this time. Have you identified the shooter?"

"Not yet," said Chase. "But we're working on it."

The man's lips tightened. This was not the message he wanted to hear. "Let me be clear. If you don't find us a shooter we're going to want to explore some other options."

"What other options?" asked Odelia.

He jerked his head in her direction. "I'm sorry, who are you again?"

"Odelia Poole. I'm a civilian consultant." She decided to keep the fact that she was also a reporter for the local newspaper under wraps for now.

He turned away from her, clearly not impressed. "Charlie has fans in high places. He's proud to count the President among them. One phone call is all it takes to get the Feds out here and poring over this attempt on Charlie's life."

"The President?" asked Odelia. "You mean, like, *the* President?"

The man turned his penetrating gaze on her. She was pretty sure he could cut glass with it. "Is there another one?" He returned his attention to Chase, whom he seemed to have identified as the man in charge. "Make no mistake, Detective. Charlie wants results. If you can't deliver him the shooter by this time tomorrow, he'll make the call. Is that clear?"

"Let me tell you something, counselor," said Chase, not the least bit intimidated by the lawyer's tactics. "When we tried to talk to Charlie and his people this morning, they brushed us off. I can't conduct this investigation without full access to both Charlie and his team. They're witnesses and it's important they give us their full cooperation. Do I have your word that you'll get them to talk to me and talk freely?"

The lawyer nodded curtly. "I'll advise them to give you full access. All the help you need." He then stuck out his hand, gave Chase a brief handshake and stalked off without offering so much as a glance or a nod in either Odelia or Uncle Alec's direction.

"Nice guy," said Chase. "Warm personality."

"Yeah, he's a real charmer," Uncle Alec agreed.

"Do you think he was bluffing?" asked Odelia. "Can he really get the Feds out here to take over the investigation?"

"Oh, I'm sure he wasn't bluffing," said Uncle Alec, rocking back on his heels. "So you better get me something, people. I don't enjoy the prospect of being locked out of my own investigation in my own town. And I definitely don't want to get in bad with the President."

"I don't want to get in bed with the President either," Chase said cheerfully.

"Wiseguy," Uncle Alec said, then wagged a finger in Chase's face. "I don't care how you do it, Kingsley, but I want results and I want them now, you hear?" He worried the few remaining hairs still desperately clinging to his scalp and sighed. "Or else we're all sunk."

CHAPTER 8

I have to admit that after our recent standoff with Diego in the alley, the three of us were feeling more than a little sandbagged. In fact it wouldn't be too much to say we were feeling punch-drunk, as if Diego had put on a pair of boxing gloves and dealt us a glancing blow—a tough proposition when you're a cat—and had knocked us KO in a single round.

As a consequence we were wandering around more or less aimlessly when suddenly a car screeched to a halt right in front of us, just as we were staggering across the road, and I realized we hadn't even looked left or right and had almost been turned into roadkill.

A head emerged from the car window, and when I looked up with a degree of trepidation, I saw that the head belonged to none other than Odelia.

"Max! Dooley! Brutus! What are you guys doing here?!" she was saying.

I knew she said this because I saw her lips moving, though the meaning of her words only hit me with a delay of a few seconds, mainly because my first thought when I saw her was that she'd told Diego she was eager to get rid of me—tired of my sad sack stalking ways.

A second head appeared, this one poking out of the driver's side of the vehicle, and I saw it belonged to Chase Kingsley, the hunky cop Odelia has been dating for a while now.

He, too, had a similar message to convey. "Brutus! Max! Dooley! What the heck?!"

Brutus, I could see, was struggling with the same reservations I was, for he hadn't forgotten that his human, too, was eager to put him out to pasture and exchange him for the latest model of feline—Diego.

Dooley, in fact, was the only one who didn't seem affected, as he sunnily announced, "We were looking for Clarice so she can help us get rid of Diego. But now that you guys are here, maybe you can help us out."

Both Chase and Odelia were silent for a beat, then they simultaneously called out, "In the car! Now!"

Of course Chase could never have understood Dooley, as he wasn't well-versed in the finer points of the feline language. He must have understood that we weren't eager to stay out in the street, though, a fact for which I was grateful. Chase might not be a Poole, but by sheer association with the Poole clan he was clearly getting there—slowly but irrevocably.

So we hopped into the pickup and made ourselves comfortable in the backseat.

Chase stepped on the accelerator and soon we were digging our claws into the creased leather to keep from being smushed against the rear. Not that Chase would mind, I ventured, as his pickup is easily as aged and decrepit as Odelia's.

I could tell from Odelia's anxious glances back at the three of us that she was eager to have a heart-to-heart. Unfortunately most humans find it strange when other humans talk to felines, so she kept her mouth shut for now. And since neither Brutus nor I were eager to talk to the very humans who were ready to put us out with the trash, silence reigned for a long beat. Until Dooley, who evidently didn't share our reservations, started singing like a canary.

"We just saw Diego in the back alley, and he told us you guys don't like us anymore. That you told him you want to get rid of us and replace us with newer models. And that you think Max is a scroungy stalker and you're sick and tired of his fat ass, and how Marge and Gran and Tex feel the same way about me and Brutus and so does Chase. Was he telling the truth, Odelia? He wasn't, was he? He was lying through his razor-sharp teeth, wasn't he?"

Odelia merely offered us a worried glance, but didn't say a word.

Chase glanced back at us through the rearview mirror, and said, "You know? It almost sounds as if he's talking to you, babe. I've never heard a cat babble as much as that one."

"Dooley," said Odelia. "His name is Dooley."

"I knew that. Hey, Dooley," he called out. "Talk some more, bud. You crack me up."

Dooley didn't need to be told twice. "Well, Diego has been charming Harriet, as usual, and Brutus doesn't like it, and neither do I. And now we want to get rid of him, just like we did the last time, so we went and tried to find Clarice, who managed to kick Diego out of Hampton Cove before and might be convinced to do it again in exchange for a lifelong supply of Cat Snax. Only we couldn't find her at her usual haunts and now we're thinking she might be hanging out at the Writer's Lodge, curled up on Dan Brown's lap—or maybe even Stephen King's or JK Rowling's—and convincing them to feature her in their next book."

"Dooley," I said, finally finding my voice again. "Please shut up. Didn't you hear what Diego said? Odelia is crazy about him. She won't like it when we try to get rid of him."

"Yeah, that stuff's a secret, Dooley," Brutus chimed in, defeating the purpose of the secret by blabbing it out to Odelia now.

My human took it all in with a shake of the head and a worried frown marring the smoothness of her brow. I could tell the conversation had rattled her.

"Hey. Now they're all talking," said Chase, still completely oblivious and liking it. "What do you think they want? Food? You think they're hungry?"

"I think they want to tell us something," said Odelia.

"Yeah—that much I understood. But what?" He glanced back at me. "You know? Wouldn't it be fun if we could understand what they are saying? I read about some professor who's developing a machine that would translate cat language into plain English. If he ever manages to get that thing operational I'm going to get me one of those. Talk to my cats."

I wanted to tell him that he didn't need to spend good money on some stupid machine. He just needed to talk to Odelia and she could tell him exactly what we were saying.

Soon we were leaving the town center, and for the first time I started to wonder where we were going. We were clearly not homeward bound. And when I saw Odelia's expression of concern, I suddenly realized exactly where we were going: to the pound!

"You guys!" I hissed. "They're taking us to the pound! Diego was right!"

"Oh, crap," said Brutus. "I knew that creep wasn't lying. We have to escape!"

"Odelia would never take us to the pound," said Dooley. "Would she?"

"Where else could they be taking us?!" I cried.

We glanced up at the windows, but they were all rolled up. And when I tried the door handle, the stupid thing wouldn't budge. We'd just have to escape the moment Chase stopped the car!

"We'll escape into the woods," Brutus said, already drawing up a plan of campaign. "If she's still alive, we'll simply join Clarice and ask her to teach us the ways of surviving in the wild."

"I've never survived in the wild, you guys," said Dooley. "I don't know if I can do it."

"Of course you can," said Brutus. "It's just a matter of… adjusting your taste."

"No more Cat Snax," I said, feeling even more dejected than before. "And no more of that delicious paté."

"Hey," said Brutus. "Cheer up, Max. If Stephen King and Dan Brown and JK Rowling are really out there, I'm sure they'll have some great snacks to dispense. Maybe they'll even adopt us. Give us a life of unparalleled pampering and luxury. Paté up the wazoo and maybe even a visit to the cat spa from time to time."

"What's the cat spa?" asked Dooley.

"It's a place where cats go to relax," Brutus explained. "I saw it on TV. They've got a playpen and a massage parlor and manicurists and hairstylists—the works. It'll be fun."

"But we won't be together," Dooley lamented.

"I don't want to go and live with Dan Brown," I said miserably. "I mean, I know I said before I wanted to star in a movie with Tom Hanks, but all I really want is to stay home with Odelia. Wake her up in the morning by sticking my nose into her armpit, help her with her articles, hang out in front of the TV and catch an episode of *The Voice* together…"

I was going to develop my theme further, but the car suddenly lurched off the road and came to a full stop in front of a large wooden gate, a man carrying what looked like a weapon of some kind giving us a penetrating scrutiny by sticking his head in the window.

"Hampton Cove PD, buddy," Chase said, and showed the man his police badge.

The guy waved us through, and Chase took us along a long and winding driveway until a large house loomed up at the end of it, and he parked in the circular driveway, crushed gravel crunching underneath his tires.

"This is it, you guys!" I said. "Let's make a run for it!"

"I don't know," said Brutus, studying the house. "It doesn't look like a pound."

"And how would you know what a pound looks like?"

"Well, not like this. Pounds usually look like the last place on earth you want to be seen in. This place? It looks like something the Kardashians would rent if they came to town."

He was right. The house we'd arrived at was one of those large McMansions, with private pools and private Jacuzzis and private cinemas in the basement and stuff. We'd seen plenty of them in the course of our investigations and this one looked just like the others.

"We're here," said Odelia after Chase had exited the car and stood stretching. She then turned to us. "Look, I don't know what Diego told you, but I have no intention of getting rid of you. When we get home I'm going to have a long talk with that cat. Secondly, I'm never going to take you guys to the pound. You're my cats and you'll always be my cats. Is that understood? Thirdly, we're here because someone has tried to shoot Charlie Dieber this morning and we're trying to figure out who did it. So do what you do best and mingle, all right? Try to talk to Dieber's cats and dogs—of which I'm sure he's got plenty—and find out what's going on." She shook her head as she shot us a look of gentle concern. "How could you possibly think I'd want to get rid of you? I love you guys so much."

Without waiting for a reply, she quickly got out and allowed us to hop down to the ground before slamming the door shut.

## CHAPTER 9

A sense of elation and warmth spread through my weary bones at Odelia's little pep talk, and suddenly it was as if life returned to its full splendor. Once again the sun shone and the birds chirped and the cloud of doom and gloom that had hung over me like a pall lifted.

"I'm sorry for ever thinking you'd abandon me, Odelia," I said as I fell into step beside my human.

"I would never abandon you, Max," she said, but when Chase gave her an odd look, she clamped her lips together.

"You know?" he said. "I could swear that sometimes you can actually talk to those cats of yours. It's the darndest thing."

She laughed. "Talk to my cats? If only. I would love that."

"Yeah. Me, too. Imagine the stuff they could tell us. For instance, they could talk to Dieber's pets and tell us what the hell is going on. Find out if the Dieber's got enemies—if people have made threats against his life and stuff."

"Yeah. If Max and Dooley and Brutus could talk—imagine how they could help us."

The three of us fell back. "We're not being put out to

pasture!" Brutus cried. Then he frowned. "I knew that cat was lying. He was trying to get into our heads. Psych us out!"

"Oh, he's nasty," I said. "Nasty and wily."

"So he was lying?" asked Dooley.

"Yep!" said Brutus. "Our humans aren't trying to get rid of us. Our humans love us! I'll bet even that big lug Chase deeply cares—even though he can't understand a meow we say."

I felt as if I were suddenly walking on air, and as I filled my lungs to capacity, I said, "Let's not disappoint Odelia. Let's show her we've got her back—just like always."

"What's the mission?" asked Dooley. "Why are we here, exactly?"

"Someone is trying to kill Charlie Dieber and we need to find out who."

"Who's Charlie Dieber?"

"He's that singer Odelia likes so much."

Dooley thought for a moment, then his face lit up. "Oh, the one who sounds like a cricket with the flu."

"That's the one."

While Chase and Odelia had walked up to the front of the house, the three of us had veered off course and were now making our way along a paved path to the back. When we arrived there, we found ourselves in a pool area, not unlike some of the other houses we'd visited in the course of our investigations. It reminded me of the house of John Paul George, the famous British pop star, and of the Kenspeckle place, the well-known reality show family. Just like at the Kenspeckles, a party was in full swing when we arrived at the back.

"Wow," said Dooley, and I think he spoke for all of us.

Music pounded from the speakers as a few dozen people were lounging around the pool, several semi-naked young women playing some kind of ball game in the water and having a blast. People were drinking, laughing, dancing and generally whooping it up. And in the center of it all, I saw a heavily tattooed Charlie Dieber sucking from a very large bong.

"What's that smell?" asked Dooley, sniffing the air. "Is that... barbecue?"

"Weed," said Brutus. "Charlie doesn't seem impressed with the attempt made on his life."

"Or maybe this is his way of trying to deal with the shock," I suggested.

Just then, Charlie shouted, "I'm coming, bitches!" and bombed into the pool, much to the amusement of the nubile girls, who quickly surrounded him like a personal harem.

"Yeah, he's clearly having a hard time coping," Brutus said. "We better spread out, you guys. Try to talk to some cats— and maybe even dogs." A look of distaste came over him as he uttered these words. Dooley and I shared the look. No cat enjoys the prospect of having to deal with the canine species. Then again, if we were to help Odelia we needed to overcome our prejudices, cat up and ferret out information where it could be found. Even if it meant having to talk to Dieber's pack of Chihuahuas or whatever foul species he favored.

So while Brutus headed towards the house, Dooley and I decided to check out the rest of the garden. And we hadn't moved ten feet when suddenly we saw a familiar face.

"Isn't that..." Dooley began.

"Clarice!" I yelled. "Yoo-hoo! Clarice!"

The feral cat was lounging on a lounge, casually licking her paws, and surveying the world with those dark eyes of hers.

"Clarice!" Dooley cried when we'd reached her. "You're alive!"

She gave him a disdainful look, her upper lip curling into

a snarl. "Of course I'm alive. Why wouldn't I be alive?"

"Diego told us you were dead. He said that he 'took care of you.'"

Her snarl tightened. "That nasty piece of work tell you that? And you believed him?"

"Well—I didn't," I told her. "I didn't believe a word he said."

Dooley stared at me. "You didn't believe him?"

"Are you kidding me? I knew he was yanking our chain. Who can take out Clarice? No one! And definitely not some hustler like Diego."

"I believed him," said Dooley. "I thought he'd killed you, Clarice. I'm glad he didn't."

"I'm very hard to kill," said Clarice, and I actually believed her.

I was so glad to see her I wanted to hug her, but of course I didn't. Hugging Clarice is one of those things you do at your own peril.

Dooley obviously liked to live dangerously, for he actually moved in for a hug. When she held up a vicious claw and produced a loud hissing sound, he quickly backed off, but didn't lose the wide grin that had appeared on his mug the moment we caught sight of her.

"You look good," I told the formerly feral cat. And she did. Usually Clarice looks like she's just been in a fight, with pieces of her mottled red fur missing and scratches across her scrawny face. One ear was still lopsided, and it was obvious someone had taken a bite out of the other one at some point. But she looked well-fed and well-tempered, her fur shiny and healthy, her cheeks full and her whiskers polished to a shine.

"Yeah, I'm one of the Dieber Babes now," she said casually, as if this was the most normal thing in the world.

We both goggled at her. "Dieber Babes?" I repeated

finally.

"What's a Dieber Babe?" asked Dooley.

"Fancats," she said. "Dieber likes cats—in fact he adores them. Collects them en masse. Calls them his Dieber Babes."

"But how—when—why?" I asked, not quite coherently. I simply couldn't imagine Clarice allowing herself to be domesticated. In fact it upset my worldview so thoroughly I suddenly felt as if I'd landed in an alternate reality. Like Neo discovering the Matrix.

Clarice shrugged. "I was hanging out at the Lodge, like I usually do, when Dieber showed up with his entourage. He needed a weekend to decompress after playing a grueling show, and decided the Lodge was the place to do it. His entourage left, and he stayed behind all by himself. And that's when we struck up a firm friendship. I would keep him company as he contemplated fate and his place in the world, and he would feed me the best damn cat food I've ever tasted in my entire life. Actual raw steak, the most delicious fish filets you can imagine, prime ribs…" Her eyes softened. "I think for the first time in my life I was in love."

"With the prime ribs?" asked Dooley.

"With a human, doofus. The guy has a way with cats. Never thought I'd ever feel that way about any human again but Charlie managed the impossible. When his retreat was over, he told me he wanted to adopt me, and I decided to let him."

"But I thought you loved your life!" I said. "Roaming around—listening to no one. Carving your own path…"

"Yeah, that all sounds great until you've actually lived it. Trust me, it's not much fun having to scrounge around for food all day long. Much easier to have some dude like Dieber provide it for you." She darted a quick look at me. "I get you now, Max. I mean, I know I've made fun of you in the past. Calling you a pansy-assed namby-pamby yellow-belly sissy, but I can see the allure of living with a human who truly cares about you. It's a pretty sweet deal."

"A Dieber Babe," I repeated. "I just—"

"What?" she asked, her eyes suddenly flashing darkly. "You gonna judge me? Huh?"

I quickly held up a peaceable paw. "Oh, no. Of course not. No judgments, Clarice. Uh-uh. I think you look great. Doesn't she look great, Dooley?"

"You look amazing," Dooley said.

Clarice smiled—the first time I'd ever seen her smile. "Thanks. I feel great. In fact I haven't felt this great in ages."

"Do you… still catch mice though, and enjoy the occasional rat?" I inquired.

She laughed. "Sure. When you've got your own private chef all you want to do is gobble up a few stinking rats."

"You've got your own private chef?" asked Dooley, eyes wide.

"Nothing but the best is good enough for Dieber's Babes," she said with a grin.

I had to hand it to her. She'd struck gold. And I was happy for her. I really was. Then again… Did she still have what it took to get rid of a certain nasty feline intruder?

"We were actually looking for you, Clarice," I said, deciding to get down to brass tacks. "Diego has been pestering us again, and I was wondering—"

"Well, talk of the devil," Clarice said, darting a pointed look behind us.

Even before I'd turned around, Diego's silky voice already rang out. "Well, who do we have here? Looks like the gang's back together again. Clarice—always a pleasure."

"The pleasure is all yours," she said with a menacing glance at the new arrival.

When I finally laid my eyes on Diego, I saw he wasn't alone. "Harriet!" I cried. "What are you doing here?"

"Oh, Max. Try to keep up," said the pretty Persian with a flash of annoyance in her green eyes. "Diego and I were invited to join Dieber's party. The real question is: what are *you* doing here?"

"Odelia brought us here," I said, raising my chin in a gesture of defiance.

"Not one of those silly murder investigations again," she said with a roll of her eyes. "When is Odelia finally going to see that cats aren't outfitted to play amateur sleuth?"

Her words were so outrageous I had a hard time coming up with a response.

"I thought you liked sleuthing, Harriet," said Dooley, giving her a somber look.

"Oh, I liked it well enough when it was all fun and games, but now it's turned into something much more sinister and I, for one, want nothing more to do with the dreadful business." She brushed a whisker. "All that death and decay. It's so depressing." She batted her eyes at Diego. "Brutus is very much into all of that stuff. Good thing you're not, Diego."

Diego visibly shivered. "You're absolutely right, babe. One shouldn't get too mixed up in the affairs of men. Let them deal with their homicidal maniacal tendencies all by themselves. Us cats should rise above that terrible habit of slaying one's brethren."

"Well spoken, darling," said Harriet. "You're so smart."

"And you're so beautiful."

"Oh, you're too sweet."

"Most beautiful babe ever. Yes, you are."

"Ooh. Kissy kissy, darling."

The cloying scene was too much for me, and I decided to remove myself before I threw up my breakfast. And as I was walking away, I saw to my surprise how Dieber himself approached, his eyes focused on but one thing: the white Persian we all knew as Harriet.

CHAPTER 10

It had taken some time for Odelia and Chase to be admitted to the house. Even though the security guard at the front gate had allowed them in, the one posted at the house had taken his time to study their credentials. It appeared as if he'd never seen a police badge before, and he'd even called Uncle Alec to check if Chase was a real cop or just some crazed fan trying to get close to the Dieber under false pretenses. When he'd started reading Chase's badge number to Odelia's uncle and giving him Chase's description, the cop had finally had enough and threatened to arrest the guy on the spot for obstruction of justice.

That had done the trick, and they'd finally been allowed to proceed.

The vestibule was large and consisted of white marble walls, floors and even ceilings. It was the life-sized horse that dominated the entrance that made Odelia draw up short. She stared at the horse, which was white and rearing up on its hind legs. On top of the horse sat an equally life-sized Charlie Dieber, his arm raised as if he was about to invade some foreign nation, his eyes fixed on the horizon and his expression dead serious.

On the side of the horse a slogan had been sprayed, which read, 'Be Who You May Be – Charlie Dieber.'

"Charlie Dieber. Philosopher," Chase murmured as he joined her. "It's a side of him I've never seen before."

"Well, he does write all of his own songs," she said.

"Of course he does."

They moved beyond Dieber the Conqueror and deeper into the house. To her surprise the place was pretty much empty. They passed through a spacious living room, where gigantic portraits on the walls announced, in case they still had doubts, that they'd entered the world of the Dieber. Six Warhol-type portraits adorned the space, each in a different bright color, and each depicting Dieber's heavily-tattooed torso. Tattoos of dollar bills, snakes and even Indiana Jones's famous fedora and whip covered every inch of skin.

Odelia gulped slightly. It was one thing to be a fan of this young man, but another to be confronted with this wealth of self-absorption and vanity. Then again, if you're going to become a global pop star, a healthy dose of egomania probably comes with the territory.

"Where is everybody?" asked Chase as they sauntered through the living room.

"They're probably in mourning," said Odelia. "Or hunkered down in the basement bunker, trying to come up with a strategy on how to deal with this attack on Charlie's life."

They entered a large kitchen, and came upon a beehive of activity—three chefs cooking up a storm while servers came and went, carrying trays and silver platters.

More trays stood on the countertops, laden with hors-d'oeuvres and other amuse-bouches, while dozens of flutes were being filled with pink champagne by rattled-looking kitchen personnel, before being snapped up by the servers and carted outside.

Noise and music had them both turn in the direction of the window, and that's when Odelia saw that a pool party was in full swing. Girls in bikinis were jumping into the pool and playing a game of water ball, while dozens of others stood rocking out to loud music.

"Um, what was that you said about Dieber being in mourning?" asked Chase.

She slowly hitched up the jaw that had dropped and stared at the scene. In light of the recent death of one of the pop star's bodyguards, this all seemed very inappropriate and more than a little disrespectful. "Maybe this is the way he deals with loss?" she tried lamely.

"Yeah, right," Chase grunted. He clearly wasn't buying it, and frankly neither was she. "Let's go outside and have a chat with our chief mourner," he suggested.

They stepped out onto the deck, and mingled with the raving crowd. The music was loud and Odelia recognized it as part of a remix of Dieber songs by the world's top DJs. She actually had the same compilation on her phone, and enjoyed listening to it at the gym.

Now she doubted if she'd ever be able to enjoy it in quite the same way again.

A freakishly muscular young man bumped up against her. "Hey, babe! Wanna get nekkid with me?"

"No, I don't want to get 'nekkid' with you," she snapped, and ignored Chase's grin.

"Wanna do some blow? Snort some coke?" the guy asked, a strange gleam in his eyes. She recognized the gleam. He was clearly high on the stuff he was hawking.

Chase held up his badge. "Police. Get lost, buddy."

In spite of his state of inebriation, the guy got the message and took a hike.

"Nice wake," said Chase. "I'm sure the family of Ray Cooper will be thrilled."

Odelia merely shook her head. And that's when she spotted the man of the hour. Charlie Dieber was seated in a lounge next to the pool, stroking... "Harriet!"

"Huh?" Chase asked.

"Look—it's my mom's cat."

He looked where she indicated, and muttered, "Well, I'll be damned. It's Diego."

Diego had belonged to Chase's mom, before she'd offloaded him on her son when her health didn't allow her to take care of him herself. And since Chase was bunking with Uncle Alec, and was rarely home, he'd asked the Pooles to look after the orange cat.

Odelia hurried over, and saw that all her cats were present and accounted for: Brutus, Dooley, Max, Harriet and Diego. Even Clarice was there, the feral cat Max had befriended.

And she'd just joined Charlie when she heard him say, "I'm adopting you, beautiful."

"No, you're not," she said, and snatched Harriet from the singer's paws. "This is my cat," she said. "Or at least my mother's."

Charlie gave her a grin. "Hey, babe. Wanna get nekkid and jump in the pool with me? I'll bet you're one hell of a swimmer."

Chase took out his badge again and flashed it in the singer's face. "Wanna get nekkid with me, douchebag? I know some great wrestling moves."

Charlie held up his hands. "Chill, dude. I'm just trying to have some fun."

"You've got a strange idea of fun—stealing someone else's cat."

"Hey, I wasn't stealing anyone's cat. I just like cats." He

smiled. "I like to call them my Dieber Babes." He gave Clarice's fur a stroke. "Isn't that right, babe?"

Clarice emitted a soft purring sound that Odelia had never heard her produce before. She looked different, too. Less mangy.

"How much do you want for the Persian?" asked Charlie now. "I want her. And what the Dieber wants, the Dieber gets."

"I'm going to have to disappoint you, Charlie," Odelia said, becoming indignant now. "Harriet is not for sale."

"She isn't, huh? How about the orange one?"

"That's my cat," said Chase, "and he's not for sale either."

"Oh, he's a he, huh? My bad. Yeah, I don't do dudes, only babes." Charlie darted a quick glance at Brutus and Dooley, but didn't seem to deem them worthy of inclusion in his harem either. "So I guess it's 'peace, out' from me then, suckers." He held up his index and middle finger, kissed them and stalked off, moving in an awkward swaying motion. He was wearing his cap with the bill backwards, and baggy pants that showed a good deal of crack. Odelia shook her head. Suddenly she wasn't so sure if she still wanted to be a Bedieber.

## CHAPTER 11

Odelia and Chase finally sat down with Carlos Roulston, the person in charge of security. Roulston was easily twice the size of Chase, who was by no means a scrawny chicken himself. Roulston's head was shaved in an intricate pattern that reminded Odelia of Egyptian hieroglyphs for some reason, and his skin was tanned to a tawny leather, his broad features stoic and unsmiling. Here sat a man who wouldn't be trifled with, she felt.

"Terrible business," the security professional intimated. "Ray was a great guy. Real team player."

They were seated in the coolness of the security head's office on the first floor. Like the man himself, the office was no-nonsense—just a desk, a couple of chairs, a small salon with coffee table and two couches, and a wall-mounted cabinet that may or may not have contained the small arsenal Charlie Dieber's security detail presumably had at their disposal. What struck Odelia was that there were no pictures of Charlie anywhere in evidence.

"So what can you tell us about threats?" asked Chase,

leaning forward. "Has anyone made any threats against Charlie's life in the recent past?"

"Dozens. There's a lot of nutcases out there, Detective, I don't have to tell you that. The moment you become famous and people write about you, the crazies come out in droves."

"You mean, like, letters, emails, social media, what?"

"All of the above." He opened a desk drawer and took out a file folder and placed it on the desk. Odelia opened it and found herself looking at a pile an inch thick of letters, cards, napkins, beer coasters, pictures, screenshots... She picked out a few and read the scribbled messages. 'You're a dead man, Dweeber.' 'I'm coming for you, singer boy.' 'We all hate you.' 'You're Satan's spawn and Jesus will wipe you out in the coming apocalypse.'

Roulston cracked his knuckles. "Like I said. There's a lot of crazies out there."

"Anything that sticks out?" asked Chase. "Anyone in particular you think might have come after your employer?"

"If you're asking me if anyone has called in and claimed responsibility for the attack, no, they haven't. And frankly I don't expect them to, either. This is some loner crackpot. A loner crackpot with a gun. Have your people determined the type of weapon that was used?"

"Colt Cobra," said Chase.

Roulston frowned. "The .38 special. That's a short-range weapon. I would have thought he was shot from a distance. Sniper style."

"No, it would appear that the killer was fairly close. Ballistics places the shooter at no more than ten feet."

Jefferson brushed his hand across his bristly buzzcut, a confused frown on his face. "Ten feet, huh? That means the shooter was in the crowd. For some reason I thought he was on the roof, scoping us out. Did you talk to the people closest to where Ray was shot?"

"We're still interviewing people. We also confiscated their phones and have downloaded all digital imagery taken at the scene."

"And?"

"So far nothing."

"That's weird. Someone must have seen something."

"There were dozens of people present, Mr. Roulston," said Odelia. "It'll take us a little time to talk to all of them, and cross-reference the witness reports."

There was a knock at the door, and four more people entered, three men and one woman. "I want to introduce you to my team," said Roulston, getting up. "Team, this is Detective Chase Kingsley—in charge of the investigation—and Odelia Poole. She's like the Rick Castle addition to the Hampton Cove Police Department if you will."

"Only I'm not a writer," Odelia quipped.

"Too bad. You could have worn one of those bulletproof vests with the word WRITER written across the front and back," said Roulston. "I want you to meet Luca Elrott, Toby Mulvaney, Jason Nugent and Regan Lightbody. They were all part of the close protection team this morning. I had more people out there, but they were in charge of crowd control."

Odelia and Chase turned their chairs around, while the foursome took a seat in the small salon. They looked downcast, which was a big difference to the hard-partying star they were all hired to protect. These people clearly cared about the man who had died.

"So what can you tell us about what happened this morning?" asked Chase.

Regan Lightbody shrugged. She was small but wiry and looked more impacted than her colleagues. "Ray was a great guy. He didn't deserve this." She glanced up, her amber eyes finding Odelia's. "You're going to find out anyway, so it's better you hear this from me. Ray and I were an item. We'd been dating on and off ever since we began working for Charlie." She darted a quick look at one of the other guards, who looked away.

Now Odelia understood why Regan seemed so crushed. "I'm sorry for your loss," she said softly.

Regan nodded and wiped at her eyes. "He was a goof, no doubt about it, but the moment we were out there he got into the zone and was the consummate professional."

"He was," Roulston confirmed. "One of the best guys I ever worked with."

There were murmurs of agreement from the others. "Yeah, Ray was a super guy. Fun to hang out with, and he always had your back," said Toby, a red-haired guy with a ready smile. "We're going to miss him."

"Did any of you catch a glimpse of the killer?" asked Chase. When they all shook their heads, he added, "Anything unusual happen? Anything out of the ordinary?"

"The shot came completely out of the blue," said Jason Nugent, a tough-looking guy with a busted nose and a sliced eyebrow. "The moment it happened we just bundled Charlie into the car and took off. I was in the car with him, so I didn't see a thing." He turned to Regan. "You stayed behind. Did you see anything?"

"Nothing. It's almost as if this guy is a ghost. All I could see were those same teens that come out every time Charlie steps out—nothing that set off any alarm bells."

"I didn't see nothing, either," said Luca in somber tones. "The thing is, when you enter this field you know that one day something like this might happen. You prepare for it, mentally and physically. But when it actually happens, like it did today? You realize nothing can prepare you." His face hardened. "We lost a friend today—a comrade. So promise me one thing, all right? You catch this bastard. You catch the bastard that did this, you hear me?"

"We hear you loud and clear, Luca," said Chase, nodding.

"We promise," said Odelia, greatly touched. "We'll find your friend's killer."

"Ray gave his life for the Dieber. The man's a hero. He deserves to get justice."

CHAPTER 12

The arrival of Diego and Harriet on the scene had dampened my initial excitement about seeing Clarice and really digging into this latest murder mystery. I'd been so eager to talk to Dieber's cat menagerie but Diego had spoiled the fun for me. It almost appeared as if he was the kryptonite to my Superman. The mere sight of him simply deflated me and robbed me of any desire to get out there and figure out who might have it in for the Dieber.

So when Odelia stepped onto the deck and gave me a nod of the head, indicating it was time to go, I was actually glad. At least I'd asked Clarice to snoop around, to which she graciously agreed. If I couldn't play Sherlock Holmes, I had a proxy who would do the honors.

On the ride back to the house, Chase's car looked more like an animal control van, minus the partition and the atmosphere of fear. There was a lot of loathing, though.

"You're a liar, Diego," Brutus was saying. "A big, fat liar and now we know."

"I wasn't lying," said Diego. "Merely easing you into a

reality you'll soon be facing. Odelia is sick and tired of you sticking to her like glue, Max. So you better be prepared."

"No, she's not," I said. "Odelia told me so herself. She'll never get rid of us. Never."

"Duh. Of course she's going to *say* that," said Diego, rolling his eyes. "She's not going to risk you running away before she drops you off at the pound and collects her fat fee."

I frowned at him. "What fat fee?"

He gave me an innocent look. "Oh, you didn't know? They pay good money for old cats. In fact they pay by the pound, so Odelia stands to get quite a fortune for you, Max."

I gasped, and cried, "Odelia! Diego says you're going to sell me by the pound!"

But unfortunately Chase was behind the wheel again, his ears pricking up at the sound of us cats duking it out, so Odelia was forced to ignore my heart cry.

"How much will she get for me?" asked Dooley softly. "I mean, I'm small, so I'm bound to fetch a lot less than Max."

"Yeah, it's almost not worth dumping you," said Diego with a dismissive glance at my friend. "And as for you, Brutus, these places pay a premium for aggressive and dangerous animals such as yourself, as they're glad to be rid of them, so you should fetch a nice bonus."

"You're full of crap, Diego," Brutus growled. "I don't believe a word you say."

"Ignore me at your peril," said Diego. "But don't come crying to me when they come for you. I'll be the one sitting pretty with my lovely girlfriend by my side."

Harriet, who'd been suspiciously quiet all through this conversation, now piped up. "Can't you do anything to convince Odelia not to do this? I mean, Max and Dooley have been my friends since, like, forever, and Brutus has come to mean a great deal to me as well."

"I don't know if she'll listen to me, babe. She's got her heart set on getting rid of the riffraff and focusing on her true treasures from now on."

"I can't listen to this," Brutus growled. "If you can't see this cat for who he truly is, Harriet, there is no hope for you."

"I'm trying to help you out here, Brutus," she snapped. "The least you can do is show me some respect."

"Respect! You threw me over for this oversized hairball and you want my respect?"

"I've earned it," she said, her tail swishing defiantly. "I was your girlfriend for a long time, Brutus. And even though we parted as friends, that doesn't mean you can talk trash about me. Furthermore, I want you to refer to me as Miss Poole from now. Only true friends call me Harriet, and judging from your recent comments you, sir, are no friend of mine."

Brutus uttered a few choice curse words that no cat should ever employ, and Dooley covered his ears with his paws, visibly aghast at the level the cat had stooped to. This conversation was clearly getting out of hand and into the gutter. Which was why it was a good thing that we had finally arrived home, and Odelia opened the door to let us out.

We instantly tripped up to the house, all of our tails held high, as a deadly silence descended over our small troupe of five.

Once inside, I immediately set paw for my bowl. Ever since Diego had stolen my food last night, I'd been worried about my disappearing stash. To my relief, Odelia had filled my bowl to the brim, and I quickly set about devouring its contents with greedy gulps before Diego had a chance to gobble it all up again. And I'd reached the bottom of my bowl when I happened to glance over, and started when Tex appeared in the kitchen, dressed in coveralls and swinging a saw in one hand and a screwdriver in the other.

"And? What do you think?" he asked cheerfully.

I joined Odelia, Chase and the other cats to stare at the latest addition to the kitchen: a small panel that had been installed in the door.

"Wow, Dad," said Odelia. "You're a fast worker."

"Idle hands are the devil's workshop, honey."

"Come on, Dooley. You be the first to try," said Odelia.

"What is it?" asked Dooley, eyeing the panel with suspicion.

"It's a pet door, you dummy," said Diego. "Here. Let me show you chumps." He took a running leap, and headed straight for the door! And to my great surprise, he didn't smash into it, but ran straight through! The panel gave way, flapped out and then in again, and Diego was gone, before returning the same way he left.

"Oh, now I see what you mean," said Dooley, and quickly followed suit. "Hey, I like this!" he exclaimed when he returned. And to demonstrate that he did, he proceeded to run three more times through the newly installed gizmo.

"Looks like a great fit, Dad," said Odelia.

"Yeah, the little fellows seem to like it," said Chase.

Harriet, quickly followed by Brutus, both passed through the door, and then it was my turn. With a happy smile, for I understood this meant I could come and go as I pleased and Odelia would save a ton on her heating bill, I headed for the pet door, stuck my head in and then… got stuck. For some reason my head went through fine, but my midsection didn't.

"Um, you guys?" I called out. "A little help?"

I felt hands fingering my belly and I giggled. I'm ticklish that way. Then those same hands pressed into my belly and slowly eased me back inside. Finally I was free, and found three humans and four cats intently staring at me, then they all burst into laughter!

"Hey! What's so funny?!" I cried. "Never seen a cat get

stuck before?"

"No, actually I haven't, Maxie, baby," said Brutus, pretty much rolling on the floor, laughing. Diego, too, was howling with mirth, and so were Harriet and even Dooley, though he tried to spare my feelings by hiding his face behind his paws.

"Very funny," I growled. I was blushing, though since I'm blorange, and covered in fur, I was pretty sure no one could see it.

"I think you're going to have to make it bigger, Dad," Odelia said finally.

"Yeah, better install an outsized pet door for an outsized cat," Chase added.

Tex scratched his scalp. "I don't think they have them in a larger size. I guess I'll have to make the next one custom-sized."

"I'll give you a hand, Tex," said Chase, clapping his future father-in-law on the back.

"Thanks, buddy," said Tex, still looking slightly stunned. "I should probably have measured Max before I got started. My mistake."

"Don't worry about it, Dad," said Odelia with a smile. "Max is a one-of-a-kind cat. He needs a one-of-a-kind pet door."

I'm not sure what she meant by that, but judging from Diego's knowing look it wasn't good. 'See?' that look seemed to mean. 'She's going to get good money for you, Max. Paid by the pound... by the pound!'

Then again, if Odelia was going to sell me by the pound to the pound, why did she go to all the trouble of installing a pet door for me? I was going to have to thresh this thing out once and for all. The moment Diego was gone I was going to have a long heart-to-heart with my human. Was she or wasn't she about to get rid of me? Inquiring minds needed to know!

## CHAPTER 13

Odelia woke up in the middle of the night from a strange noise bleating away in the vicinity of her ear. For a moment she thought it was Max, whose breathing could get a little noisy from time to time, especially when he was having a bad dream. He would start to paw the air, as if running in his sleep. She'd asked Vena, her veterinarian, about it once and she said he was probably dreaming about chasing something or being chased himself.

The notion that cats could dream had been a new one for her, but it didn't surprise her. In fact there wasn't much about her cats that did surprise her these days. They were amazing creatures, and capable of so much more than most humans gave them credit for.

They were also very sensitive. As she was falling asleep earlier, Max had tripped up to her, carefully looking left and right, and had asked her if it was true that she intended to drop him off at the pound one of these days, and actually sell him by the pound. The idea was so outrageous that she'd laughed it off. But when he told her the story had been launched by Diego, it wasn't all that funny anymore. It would appear that Diego had been feeding Max and the others a bunch of sensationalist stories, and scaring them witless in the process.

So she'd impressed it upon Max that she had no intention whatsoever to sell him to any pound, and vowed to have a long talk with Diego and tell him to stop this nonsense.

She reached out and took her phone from the nightstand and saw that it was Chase.

Picking up, she groggily muttered, "Mh?"

"Very eloquent, Poole," Chase's voice came. He sounded more awake than she was. "There's been an incident at the Dieber place. Some lunatic placed a knife on Charlie's pillow, and now he's scared out of his feeble little mind and has been yelling for cops, cops, cops!"

"So? I'm not a cop. You go."

"Outside. Five minutes. Oh, and Odelia?"

"Huh?"

"You sound sexy when you're sleep-deprived."

Five minutes later she was outside, trying to rub the sleep from her eyes, and watched Chase's big pickup drive up, the engine rumbling pleasantly, the burly cop looking as fresh as a daisy. How did he do it? He gave her a big grin as he pushed open the door. She dropped into the seat and immediately leaned her head against the headrest and fell asleep.

A prod woke her up again. "Look alive, champ. We've arrived."

She wrenched open her eyes and stretched her arms out as much as the cramped space in the cabin would allow. "So what's this story about Dieber finding a knife?"

"That *is* the story. Dieber found a knife on his pillow."

"So what's the deal? Is it a threat? Was there a note? What?"

"That's what we're here to find out, babe." He gave her a

look of concern. "Are you sure you're up for this? You look like you crawled out from under a steamroller."

"Had a long talk with Max before nodding off," she muttered before catching herself. "I mean—Max kept me awake half the night."

"He probably wasn't happy that he couldn't fit through the pet door. Don't worry. I'll give your dad a hand tomorrow and we'll fix it."

She glanced over. "How come you're so... chipper? What's your secret?"

He shrugged his broad shoulders. "No secret. I tend to wake up at the drop of a hat ready to go. Always have."

"You don't feel like a zombie fresh from the grave?"

"Nope."

"And you don't need a gallon of coffee before you're ready to start your quest for brains?"

"Nope. Though coffee would be welcome. I hope the Dieber got a fresh pot brewing."

"You're something else, Detective Kingsley."

"Just your friendly neighborhood cop, always ready for duty, ma'am."

They'd arrived at the gate to the Dieber compound, and the same guard who'd admitted them the day before was on duty. This time he recognized them, and waved them through without delay. Chase parked his rig in front of the house, and they trudged up to the front door. That is to say, Odelia trudged. Chase bounced athletically on limber legs.

Once inside, they were greeted by a scene of extreme pandemonium. No semi-naked girls prancing around in the pool this time, but guards and girls and staff members running around like headless chickens, and Charlie Dieber having a major freak-out in the living room—the one with the six Warhol-type portraits of his tatted-up torso.

"They're trying to get me!" he was screaming. "But I won't

be gotten! Nobody can kill the Dieber. The Dieber is invincible. The Dieber is indestructible! The Dieber is bulletproof!"

"I hate it when they talk about themselves in the third person," Chase said.

"Me, too," she intimated.

The Dieber finally caught sight of the twosome and his face lit up. "Cops!" he cried. "I need cops, cops, cops!"

"Well, you got them, Charlie," said Chase. "Now what's all this about a knife?"

The Dieber dropped the vape he'd been sucking from into the hands of a plump woman dressed as a housekeeper, and stalked up to them. As usual, he was shirtless, wearing only Bermudas, and his bare feet slapped the marble floor. He tapped Chase's chest with his finger, getting into the cop's face. "Someone left a knife on my pillow. A frigging knife! So what are you going to do about it, huh? The Dieber could have died tonight!"

"I guess I'll take a look at the knife," Chase said with a tight smile.

The Dieber returned to pacing the living room, and Odelia didn't know what was more unnerving, watching his Bermudas drop a little lower with every step and show a bare bottom that was as inked up as the rest of his body, or the fact that the killer had gotten so close to the star that he could have slit his throat if he wanted to.

Carlos Roulston was there, and so were the members of Charlie's close protection team, and they escorted Odelia and Chase up a sweeping flight of stairs and into a bedroom that was easily as large as Odelia's entire house. In fact it was safe to say Charlie's bedroom was the size of a luxury suite and resembled one as well. The four-poster bed stood near the window, overlooking the ocean, and once again portraits of the pop star were the main decoration. The man was clearly in love with himself. There was also another white horse, rearing up with the Dieber seated on its back. Only this time the Dieber was in the nude.

She averted her gaze, suddenly feeling she'd already seen too much of the kid, and joined the guard detail around the singer's bed, where the knife was still very much in evidence on the pillow, as indicated. Almost like a pillow chocolate, but with an edge.

"We talked to the housekeeper," said Roulston. "She says that when the cleaners were in here there was no knife."

"When was this?" asked Chase.

"This morning at ten, and again at ten tonight."

"They come in twice a day?"

"Yup. Charlie is a neat freak. Wants fresh sheets put on his bed twice a day."

"But… why?" asked Odelia.

Roulston shrugged. "Let's just say this bed sees a lot of… action."

"Oh." She decided not to ask him to elaborate.

"So the knife must have been put here between the time the cleaners left and the time Charlie turned in for the night," said Chase. "Which was… when, exactly?"

"According to Charlie he got up here at around three. Before that, he spent time in the private recording studio in the basement, working on his music. Then he went for a dip in the pool with some of his Bediebers—the girls who permanently live on-site—and when he got here with three of them—"

"He's a horny little devil, isn't he?" said Chase.

"He is blessed with a healthy libido," Roulston admitted with a slight grin.

"So they got here, and then what?"

"Charlie saw the knife and freaked—screaming bloody murder. He's been at it since."

Odelia walked up to the bed and studied the knife. It was

just your regular garden-variety kitchen knife. No note, no threatening words scribbled on the wall, no nothing.

"Interesting," said Chase, scratching his scalp. "Any idea who could have done this?"

Roulston shook his head. "Must be one of the staff. The house is locked down at night, no one allowed in or out. I've got people guarding the perimeter, and I've hired more guards to make sure no one can get near the house or Charlie."

"You're saying this was an inside job."

"Has to be. Whoever placed this knife was already on the premises."

"One of Charlie's girls, maybe? Jealous of one of the others?"

"We've talked to all of them. They don't seem particularly attached to Charlie—simply happy for the opportunity to be close to a rich superstar and bask in the benefits."

Chase nodded. "We're going to want to talk to everyone on staff. Housekeepers, cleaners, drivers, chefs, servers, the pool boy—if you have a pool boy."

"We have a pool girl," Roulston said.

"Of course you do. I'll call in some more colleagues, and we'll start the interviews."

And so it went down. Chase called Uncle Alec, who called more of his people, and for the next two hours they went through the full roster of Charlie Dieber's staff, which was even more extensive than Odelia had imagined. The guy clearly believed in living the good life.

At least there was coffee. Plenty of coffee. And then she settled in for the duration and assisted Chase in interviewing the two dozen people who might have issued the threat.

## CHAPTER 14

I was singing my heart out, and finally starting to feel like myself again. It was cat choir night, and I was flanked by Dooley and Brutus as I took my place in the choir and joined in the fun. Shanille, our principal conductor, was swinging her paws just so, and for a moment I forgot all my troubles as I belted out cat choir tunes with reckless abandon.

Cat choir gathers in Hampton Cove Park and is one of my favorite social gatherings. Practically every Hampton Cove cat is a member, and it's the place to be in town once the sun goes down. All around us, night had fallen, which never bothers us one bit, since, as you may or may not know, the feline eyesight is a great deal superior to the human eyesight.

The only minor issue marring this wonderful time for us were the humans who live around the park and who enjoy yelling abuse at us. They obviously weren't fans of music.

And we were just launching into *Uptown Girl*—Billy Joel is a local and a fan favorite—when two new arrivals disturbed my equanimity. They were none other than Harriet and... Diego.

Harriet had always been a member of cat choir, but hadn't attended ever since she started seeing Diego. Probably since Diego had never been invited. Who would invite him? Not me, and definitely not Brutus or Dooley.

When our moving rendition of the Billy Joel hit was done —basically all of us screeching as hard and as loud as we could, and Shanille trying to impose a measure of harmony, Diego clapped his paws. "Beautiful!" he exclaimed. "Wonderful! Such talent!"

Shanille seemed touched. "Why, thank you, Diego. I'm so glad you could make it."

"Wait, what?" I asked. "You invited this cat?"

"Of course I invited Diego," said Shanille. "He'll be a great admission to cat choir."

"But... the first rule of cat choir is... you do not talk about cat choir!" said Brutus.

"Unless a rare talent like Diego turns up," Shanille insisted.

The other cats murmured in agreement, and all around I could sense the mood shifting. They were all looking at Diego as if he was the second coming of Christ, and Brutus, Dooley and I were the Judases standing in the cat's way. Even Shanille was giving us a look of disapproval. "Go easy on them, Shanille," Diego said. "They're good cats. Just... no talent."

"What?!" I cried. I turned to Shanille. "You're not listening to this nonsense, are you?"

"I'm sorry, Max. I talked this through with Diego, and I have to agree. The three of you lack the required talent to be in our choir. I always knew something was amiss, I just didn't know what it was. It took Diego to figure out what was wrong with our sound. It's you, Max. And Brutus and

Dooley. You... well, I'm just going to say it—the three of you can't sing."

I gawked at the cat. "You can't be serious."

"What is she talking about, Max?" asked Dooley.

"She's... kicking us out!"

"You can't kick us out," said Brutus. "I just became a member."

"I'm afraid Diego is right. Cat choir should be a place for the enjoyment of music. Only cats with a musical bone in their bodies are welcome. And I'm afraid you three don't have what it takes." She sighed deeply. "It is with great regret, therefore, that I must ask you to leave."

"You can't do this," I said. I pointed at Diego. "He's evil!"

"This hurts me more than it hurts you, Max," said Diego mournfully. "But we have to think of cat choir. I'm sure you'll agree with me that the needs of the many outweigh the needs of the few."

"Here, here," one cat called out.

"Well spoken, Diego!" cried another.

"Diego is right," said Shanille. "He will take your place, and I'm sure he'll do great."

"Bye-bye, Max," said Diego. "And don't feel bad. We can't all be as talented as me."

"I'm going to get you for this," Brutus growled as he took a menacing step in Diego's direction. "I swear to God—"

"No violence, please, gentlecats," said Shanille, holding up a conciliating paw. "And no blasphemy. If you have any respect for cat choir, you will accept the decision of the majority."

I turned to the others. "You don't want us gone, do you? I've known you guys forever!"

But they all gave me a stony-faced look. It was clear Diego had gotten to them, too. And then Diego cried, "And just like I promised, Cat Snax for everyone! My treat!"

"You bought them with Cat Snax," I said, now truly in shock. "You bribed them."

"To celebrate the arrival of this exciting new talent, Diego has indeed agreed to dispense a little treat amongst the members," said Shanille, lifting her chin. "No bribery involved whatsoever. Merely a small token of his appreciation."

Harriet gave us a look of commiseration, but then turned away. It was obvious which side she'd chosen in this escalating cat war.

"Come on, Max," said Brutus. "We're not welcome here anymore."

And as we stalked off, Dooley said, "I liked cat choir. I really did."

"Me too, buddy," I said. "In fact I loved it."

"You know?" asked Brutus. "You and I had some issues when I first arrived in town, Max. But never like this. Never like Diego."

"No, never like Diego," I agreed. "That cat is pure evil."

"We have to talk to Clarice," said Dooley. "She's the only one who can save us."

"At least Odelia is not selling us to the pound, you guys," I said as we left the park and convened on the sidewalk, under a streetlamp, for an impromptu crisis meeting.

"She's not?" asked Dooley.

"Nope. I talked to her and she said it's all rubbish. She would never sell us or get rid of us. Diego has been talking through his hat. It's all lies. Filthy lies to get our backs up."

"Unless he's right and Odelia is lying," said Dooley.

"Who's the more likely liar?" asked Brutus. "Diego or Odelia?"

Dooley thought about this for a moment but finally gave up. "Is that a trick question?"

"Diego, of course!" Brutus cried. "Odelia wouldn't lie to us. Would she, Max?"

"No, she would not," I said, coming to my human's defense. "She's never let me down before, and she won't now. She said she would talk to Diego, and I hope she does."

"Fat lot of good that'll do," said Brutus, his skeptical nature shining through. "I mean, Diego is such a great con artist he'll simply wrap her around his little finger again." He pounded his paw with his other paw. "No, we need to fix this ourselves, you guys. Or, better yet," he added, gesturing at Dooley, "talk to Clarice again. She will fix this for us."

And so we set out to Charlie Dieber's place again. It was a long hike, but since we didn't have anything better to do, we accepted our fate with equanimity. The nocturnal trek soon soothed the bitter memory of Diego kicking us out of cat choir, and when we finally arrived at the large compound the Dieber occupied, the fresh ocean breeze and the relative quiet of the night had done its healing work and I was starting to feel a little better again.

We met Clarice out on the deck, where she sat gazing up at the full moon as it cast its pale light across the world. She looked forlorn, but that was probably just my imagination.

"Hey, Clarice," I said by way of greeting. "Fancy meeting you here."

She barely glanced up. "Oh, it's you again."

I would have hoped for a little more enthusiasm, but at least she didn't kick us out.

We joined her, and Brutus said, "Great night, huh? The moon… the stars… the, um, trees…"

"Oh, cut the crap, Brutus," she said. "What do you want?"

"We never finished that conversation about Diego," said Brutus, not discouraged.

"We need to get rid of Diego again, Clarice," I explained. "And we can't do it alone. We need your help. You got rid of him so magnificently last time, and we wanted to ask you to do it again."

"As a favor to us," Brutus said. "Because that cat is making our lives a living hell."

Clarice was still staring up at the moon. "I'd always wondered, you know," she said softly.

"Wondered what?" I asked.

"What life would be like for a cat like you. Having a human who loves you—takes care of you—takes you to the vet to deworm you and all."

I drew myself up to my full height. "I'll have you know I've never had to be dewormed."

"You know what I mean." She sighed. "This place is such a madhouse. Two dozen cats living in the same house. Can you imagine? It's driving me nuts. Out there in the woods I had my own space. Peace and quiet. No one to bother me. Here? Yackety-yackety-yackety-yack all day and all night long." She shook her head. "I like the food, and I like Charlie, but his pack of cats is too much. This may sound crazy but I'm starting to think about getting out of here."

"So what about Diego?" asked Dooley, never one to apply tact or diplomacy.

Clarice turned a pair of fierce eyes on Dooley and he visibly shrank into his fur. "Who do you think I am? Your personal bitch? I don't take orders from no one, buster. Least of all some pampered little—" She caught herself and grimaced. "Oh, my. Who's the pampered one now, huh? I guess the joke's on me for calling you guys names all these years."

"I'm sorry you feel this way, Clarice," I said, shooting Dooley a cautionary look.

"Yeah, that makes two of us," she said, returning her gaze to the moon, which for some reason she'd developed a fascination with. "Look, I'm not your mother. If you have some issue with Diego you'll just have to handle it. You're big cats. You don't need me."

"But Clarice!" Dooley cried. "He's just kicked us out of cat choir!"

"Who cares about cat choir? Cats can't sing. Everybody knows that."

"We can sing just fine," I said, feeling hurt. This was the second time in a single night that my singing abilities had been questioned and I wasn't sure I liked it.

"Look, I took care of Diego once. I'm not doing it again. I've got no beef with that cat. So if you want to get rid of him you're just going to have to cat up and do it yourselves."

Just then, there was a commotion on the upstairs balcony, and to my great surprise I suddenly saw Odelia and Chase briefly appear, before returning indoors.

"Hey! What's Odelia doing here?" I asked.

"Oh, some idiot left a knife on Charlie's pillow," said Clarice dismissively. "And now the whole house is in the throes of some great pandemonium. It's one of the reasons I'm thinking about splitting. I can't even think with all the noise and the drama."

"Who put the knife there?" asked Dooley.

"One of the security guards," said Clarice. "Luca something. He must have thought it was some big joke. But Charlie isn't laughing, and neither am I, for that matter."

"I'll bet this Luca is real sorry now, huh?" asked Brutus.

"Nobody knows it was him," said Clarice. "One of the cats told me. She saw Luca put the knife on Charlie's pillow and then stalk off again. I would have told Charlie but unlike your human Charlie doesn't understand us. Which is weird for a self-proclaimed cat lover."

I slowly raised my eyes to the balcony. I had to tell Odelia. She probably didn't have a clue about this Luca character placing the knife on Charlie's pillow. It was a great scoop.

"Thanks, Clarice," I said, and started towards the house.

"Hey! Where are you going?" asked Brutus.

"I have to talk to Odelia!" I called back.

"What about Diego?!"

"I'm sorry! Duty calls!"

"Cats," I heard Clarice mutter. "Can't live with them—can't kill them."

CHAPTER 15

Odelia rubbed her eyes. Sucking down three cups of coffee in a row that a friendly housekeeper had brought her wasn't helping. They'd interviewed most of the household staff and all of the security personnel, and so far they had nothing. Bupkis. Nada.

No one had seen anything—no one knew anything. And Dieber was getting more and more antsy with every passing minute. Every few seconds he stuck his head in and asked if they'd found his killer yet. She would have liked to point out that in order for there to be a killer in the house he would have had to be killed first, but bit her tongue.

"This is getting us nowhere," she told Chase when they'd interviewed an actual butler. The man had been hired to welcome the guests in case Charlie threw one of his parties, but since the incident the security team had taken over and introduced a more stringent vetting procedure and the man was essentially out of work. The fact that he was still on staff indicated Charlie either had way too much money to burn or was a true philanthropist. Odelia suspected the former.

"Someone must have seen something," Chase insisted.

She decided she needed a break, and went in search of a bathroom. They'd conducted their interviews in one of the guest bedrooms, but the one they'd picked didn't have an ensuite bathroom. And she'd just walked out of the facility, after having splashed some water on her face, when none other than Max came trotting up the white marble staircase, visibly out of breath, and yelling excitedly, "Odelia! I know! I know who did it!"

She crouched down, checked if no one was around, and asked, "What are you doing here?"

"Long story—no time," he said between gasps. "The guy who planted the knife is called Luca and he's a security guard. One of the cats saw him and told Clarice and Clarice told us, and now I'm telling you." He took a deep breath. "Luca. Knife. He's the killer, Odelia!"

She smiled and rubbed him behind the ear. "You did good, Max. I think you just might have solved the case."

He gave her a pleading look. "So now can I stay? You're not going to sell me to the pound?"

She groaned. This Diego was doing a real number on her cats. "I told you already, Max. I'm never going to sell you to anyone. You're my cat and that'll never change."

She thought he actually smiled at this, though it was hard to be sure with all the hair.

"Thanks. Oh, and say hi to Chase from me."

"For obvious reasons I won't," she said with a grin, getting up. "Oh, and if you want a treat, the cat food is laid out in the kitchen pantry. It's being replenished twenty-four-seven, so I'm sure you'll find what you need."

"Thanks, Odelia," he said a little breathlessly, and gave her a look of such adulation she had to laugh.

"Dig in," she said. "You've earned it." She hurried back to the bedroom where Chase was now staring out the window at the pool, its lights giving it an eerie glow. She stopped short of blurting out her exciting discovery when she realized she couldn't tell him about Max. So how to handle this? She decided to play it cool.

He turned when he heard her approach. "So who's next?" he asked.

She made a display of checking her notes. "Have we talked to Luca Elrott yet?"

He frowned. "Remind me. Who is he again?"

"We saw him in Roulston's office. He's part of Charlie's protection detail."

"Oh, right. I remember. Well, since Roulston talked to his people we can skip him."

"I... I have a hunch, Chase," she admitted. "I think we need to talk to the guy."

He gave her a funny look. "A hunch, huh? By all means then, call him in."

"Thanks," she said gratefully. There had been a time when Chase would have made fun of her hunches, but after having worked more than a few cases together, he knew how valuable they were. So she got on the horn with Roulston, and conveyed her request.

Luca Elrott was a man with a concave face, as if someone had once hit him with a football and his face had never bounced back. He had a flat nose, and eyes set too close together. The effect was a little disconcerting, like watching a cartoon character come alive.

"Hi, Luca," said Chase, taking a seat at their makeshift interview table—a nice vanity table with the mirror removed. "Come on in. We just got a couple of questions for you."

"I answered all of Roulston's questions," said Luca, sitting down across from them.

"Yeah, well, we like to be thorough," said Chase. "A very serious incident took place here tonight, and we need to figure out who's responsible."

"Of course. I understand, Detective."

He didn't look particularly at ease, Odelia thought, and wondered how she was going to make this man confess. She could hardly go with 'The cat saw you!'

Why would Luca want to murder his employer? He had to have a motive. Maybe a monetary one? Or could he be working for some mysterious cabal that wanted Charlie dead?

She listened as Chase asked all the usual questions, and the guy answered them all without a hitch. Suddenly she had it. She knew how she could make him talk.

She cleared her throat. "You were seen, Luca."

"Huh?" he said, shifting his eyes from Chase to her.

"When you planted that knife? Someone saw you."

"Who?"

She smiled. "An innocent man wouldn't ask who. He would cry out his innocence."

He shifted in his seat. "Yeah, I mean I didn't do it, so whoever saw me is lying."

"No, they're not. Why did you do it, Luca? Why did you try to kill Charlie?"

"Are you crazy? I just told you I didn't do it!"

"Look, we've established that you did, so now all I need to hear from you is why."

"But—"

"We can cut you a deal, Luca. If you tell us who you're working for. If not, you'll go away for a very long time for the murder of Ray Cooper."

The man's eyes went wide. "But I didn't kill Ray! We were best buds! He got me this job—you can ask anyone. I've known Ray since high school. We played ball together."

"All the more reason to tell us who paid you to take that shot," said Chase. He rubbed the back of his neck. "Look,

Luca. I've got the warrant for your arrest right here." He patted a folded-up piece of paper on the vanity. It contained a blueprint of the house, but Luca didn't need to know that. "All signed and ready to go. Judge wasn't happy being dragged out of bed in the middle of the night, but when we showed him the witness statement he was more than willing to sign. So we know you did it. Now all we need to know is who paid you."

Luca looked torn for a moment, then shook his head. "Look, I didn't kill Ray, all right? I'm not lying. He was my best friend. It's just that…"

"It's just what?" asked Chase, shooting Odelia a look of surprise.

Luca exploded. "Charlie is such a knucklehead! Some idiot shot Ray and all he can think about is his next party? Jump in the pool with his Bediebers? Come on! Show some respect, dude! A good man just took a bullet for you, and you're sucking on your bong and hitting the pool? I just wanted to teach him a lesson, you know. Make him sit up and think."

"So… you didn't kill Ray?" asked Odelia.

"Of course not! We were like brothers!"

"But you did place the knife," said Chase.

"Yeah, I did. I just wanted to scare the douchebag a little. He's such a prick."

Odelia believed him, and so apparently did Chase, for he gave the man a stern look and said, "I understand why you did it, Luca, but your behavior is still intolerable for a man hired to protect and serve. You can see that, right?"

"It's tough to protect and serve a man like Charlie Dieber, Detective. A man who deserves no respect whatsoever."

"I get that. But you knew that going in. The least you could do is act like a professional."

Odelia thought he was going to add, 'Dismissed,' but instead he called in Roulston.

"So am I under arrest now?" asked Luca, gesturing at the 'arrest warrant.'

"Nope. But I think it's safe to say your services will no longer be required."

"You know what? That's actually a relief," said Luca. He then gave Chase and Odelia a pleading look. "Please find Ray's killer. He was a good man. He didn't deserve to die."

Chase clapped a hand on the man's shoulder. "We will find his killer, Luca. You have my word on that."

They watched as Roulston escorted him out. The moment the two men were gone, Chase turned to her. "How did you know he was the one?"

She shrugged. "Like I said. Just a hunch."

"Just a hunch, huh? You've got some great hunches, Poole."

"Thanks for trusting me, Chase," she said, and she meant it.

"You know what your uncle told me when I first came to town?"

"No, what?"

"If my niece tells you something, you better listen."

"Is that why you gave me such a hard time?"

He grinned. "I'll admit, I was an idiot."

"Yes, you were."

"He was right, though. You're something else, Odelia Poole."

She placed her hands around his neck, and they shared a quick kiss.

They still hadn't found Ray Cooper's killer—in fact they were nowhere near solving this case—but somehow she had a hunch they were finally getting somewhere.

CHAPTER 16

*D*ooley, Brutus and I were on our way home, and when I told them about my little chat with Odelia, and how she'd assured me once more that she wasn't secretly planning to get rid of us, they were happy as clams.

"See? I told you," said Brutus. "Diego is a liar. That's all there is to it. No way would Odelia or her folks ever kick us out. They adore cats! They love us!"

"I'm so glad," said Dooley. "I feel so relieved. In fact I think I'm going to cry."

I patted his little head. "It's okay, Dooley. Let it all out, buddy. Don't hold back."

"Now all we need to figure out is how to dislodge Diego from the house," said Brutus.

"And from cat choir," I added. "I don't take being kicked out of cat choir lightly."

"We need to get that cat out of town, out of our lives, out of existence!" Brutus said.

"But how?" asked Dooley, sniffling and licking his nose. "Clarice won't help us."

"Yeah, that's a serious setback," Brutus agreed. "A very serious setback indeed."

And we were so busy contemplating ways and means of getting rid of Diego that we didn't even notice that a white stretch limousine had approached us from behind and had come to a full stop right next to us. The door opened, a hand stole out, and quickly grabbed me by the neck and hauled me inside! Next were Brutus and Dooley, and we found ourselves staring at none other than… Charlie Dieber!

He was smiling at us, sucking from a vape. "Hello, lovely ladies. Have we met?"

For a moment there I thought he could talk feline, but when I said, "Yeah, we met. You told me you don't do dudes, dude—only babes."

He grinned like an idiot, then had a fit of the giggles. "It's almost as if you're actually talking to me!" he said between two snorts.

"What is this guy smoking?" asked Brutus.

"I don't know but it's not nicotine," I said.

"News flash, cats," said the Dieber, having recovered slightly. He was now lying on his back, staring up at the limo ceiling, which, to my surprise, featured a large picture of Dieber's face. Huh. "I'm going to adopt you," he continued. "Add you to my squad. I think you three lovely ladies will fit right in. You," he added, sticking a finger in my belly, "are a big fatty, and big fatties are usually not my style, but on you it looks kinda cute. And I dig it, girl!"

"Yeah, I dig you, too, buddy," I said. "But here's another news flash: I already belong to someone."

"We all do," said Brutus.

"Guys, I don't think he speaks cat," said Dooley.

"And he seems to think we're female," I said.

"Hey, driver!" the Dieber called out. "Plot a course for Dieber Castle, my faithful retainer!"

The driver glanced back, and when he saw the three of us did a double take. The car swerved across the road for a moment before he took control again. "Um, boss?"

"Speak now or forever hold your peace!" Charlie cried and giggled again.

"Those cats?"

"Real beauties, aren't they? I love it when I can save a few strays."

"They're males, boss."

"Good one, driver. You are a very funny individual."

"For real, boss. I know cats, and those cats are definitely male. Just look at the faces."

Charlie did his utmost to focus on my visage, blinking a few times in the process. He clearly had a hard time clearing the mist his suspicious vape had caused. "I like her face," he said. "Good, strong features. Nice coloring, too. Orange."

"Blorange," I said.

"Not *her* face, *his* face," the driver insisted. "Male cats have broader features than females, whose faces are more narrow. And look at the size of that cat. The sucker's huge!"

"I know, right? And normally I don't go for the chubby ones but there's something about this one that holds a certain appeal to me. No idea why that would be the case."

"And look at the black one. If that's not a male I'm eating my hat, boss!"

"You mean the ugly one? I'm only taking him in cause I'm feeling charitable." He stared at Brutus for a moment, then frowned. "You know? You might be right. I don't get a feminine vibe from that one. If I didn't know any better I'd swear he's ready to pounce."

"Oh, I'm ready to pounce, buster," said Brutus. "Calling me ugly? I'm not ugly!"

"Yuck," suddenly said Charlie, rearing back. Then he screamed, "Stop the car!"

The car lurched to a stop and we tumbled from our perch. Before I knew what was happening, I found myself whizzing through the air. The next moment I landed—on my paws, I might add—in a ditch. In spite of my perfectly executed landing, momentum carried me on, and finally I came to a full stop with my head in a patch of nettles. There was a soft thump, and something bumped into my rear. When I managed to extract my head from the nettles, I saw that it was Dooley. Another bump, and Brutus crash-landed on top of the both of us.

I groaned as I listened to Charlie's limo driving away with screeching tires, Charlie hollering over the noise, "No dudes, dudes! Only babes for Charlie!" Then he was gone.

"He kicked us out," Brutus said, disentangling his limbs from ours with some effort. "The little dweeb actually kidnapped us and then kicked us out of his car."

"I don't think he likes male cats," Dooley intimated as he checked if he was still in possession of all of his body parts.

"No, he does not," I said. "Which is probably a good thing. Imagine having to live with two dozen cats and that maniac."

"At least we'd be rid of Diego," said Dooley. "Though I still prefer to live with the Pooles."

"Yeah, me, too," said Brutus. "Life with Charlie Dieber is way too stressful for me."

We made our way out of the ditch—which fortunately for us was devoid of sludge or water—and climbed up to the road. We looked left and right, making sure the Dieber limo wasn't about to run us over, and continued our long trek home.

"You know?" asked Dooley as we traversed a field. "Why didn't we ask Odelia for a ride?"

Brutus and I shared a dumbfounded look. Dooley was right. Why hadn't we thought of that? It would have saved us a long hike. Then again, this breath of fresh air was doing me a world of good. And as we walked on, laughing about our recent Dieber adventure, I suddenly started feeling happy for no particular reason. Maybe because in spite of Diego's machinations the three of us still had each other's backs. Cat choir might have thumbed its nose at us, but it had strengthened our bond. Now if only we could get rid of Diego…

## CHAPTER 17

On their way home, Chase passed Brown's Apothecary, the 24-hour pharmacy, and she said, "Just drop me off here, Chase. I just thought of something."

"Another hunch, huh?"

"Something like that."

"If you need aspirin, I've got some at home."

"No, it's nothing. I just need to pick something up for my cats."

"All right," he said. "You sure love those furballs of yours, don't you?"

"Yeah, I do," she admitted. He pulled up to the curb and she got out.

"Aren't you forgetting something?" he asked, leaning over.

"Um, pretty sure I'm not."

"You've got a smudge on your nose, Poole. C'mere."

She stuck her head back in, wondering where she could have smudged her nose, and when she was close enough he gave her nose a kiss. "There. That should take care of it."

"I, um, I think I have another one... here," she said, pointing at her upper lip.

He quickly pulled her into the cab and she laughed as he ravished her until they both had to come up for air. "Well, hasn't this been fun?" he asked with a grin as she crawled from his lap and out of the car. "We should do this again sometime."

"See you around, Chase."

"Pick you up in the morning?"

"Sure thing. Though you're going to need a cannon to wake me up."

He drove off and she headed into the pharmacy. Max and Dooley had been looking so dispirited lately she thought they could use some extra vitamins. Max probably thought it was the beef he seemed to have with Diego, but she was pretty sure he simply needed some choice supplements. Or maybe she should change his diet? Max was a very picky eater.

She got the vitamins and walked out of the pharmacy, and she'd just set foot for home when a white stretch limo drew up next to her and Charlie Dieber opened the door.

He was only dressed in navy star-spangled boxers and looked much the worse for wear. Not the squeaky-clean pop star she'd become a fan of. "Hey, babe!" he called out from inside the limo. The pervasive sweet smell of marijuana assaulted her nostrils and she coughed. "Wanna party with the Dieber?"

"No, thank you," she said with a disapproving frown. "And shouldn't you be home?"

"Home's for suckers," he announced. "Besides, they keep trying to kill me, so home's kinda dangerous right now. But I've got everything we need right here, babe. Just step into the Dieber Machine and the Dieber will give you a night you will never forget."

She bent down so her eyes were level with the pop star's. "I'm Odelia Poole, Charlie."

He grinned lasciviously. "Nice to meet you, Odelia Poole. Lovely name for a sexy dame."

"I'm working with the police to find the man who tried to shoot you this morning."

"I'm liking you better and better. Why don't you get in so you can tell me all about it?"

"She's a cop, boss," the driver called out. "You may want to rethink this."

Charlie gulped. "A cop? She doesn't look like a cop. Are cops usually this hot?"

"She's a civilian consultant," said the driver, who seemed to be well-informed.

"We met at the house this afternoon," Odelia reminded him, a touch of pique in her voice. How could this idiot not recognize her? They met twice! "And again this evening? I was the one who discovered it was one of your bodyguards who put that knife on your pillow?"

"So you did!" he said, his face clearing. "Hey, you're clever *and* hot!"

She pressed her lips together. "Please be on your way, Charlie." She would have said 'Please get lost,' but she was still working the man's case, and didn't want to be rude.

"Ouch." He touched his bare chest. "You just broke the Dieber's heart, babe."

"Oh, for crying out loud," she muttered, slammed the limo door shut and stalked off.

He rolled down his window. "Some other time, huh, babe? Can I have your number?"

Without turning back, she held up a hand. She would have raised her middle finger but the same principle still applied: never disrespect the subject of an ongoing investigation.

She couldn't help wondering, though, if the world

wouldn't be a better place if Charlie Dieber had taken that bullet that morning instead of Ray Cooper. She reprimanded herself. Charlie might be a douchebag, but even douchebags didn't deserve to die. Right?

## CHAPTER 18

After a long trek, we finally made it back to Hampton Cove. We passed through the small marina, the streets pretty much deserted, as one would expect in the middle of the night, and that's just the way we liked it. And we were about to head on home and sample some of that delicious kibble our humans like to put out when Brutus froze midstep, and stared straight ahead, like a pointer dog—which is odd, since Brutus doesn't even like dogs.

"What's wrong, Brutus?" asked Dooley, ever considerate.

"This is the end," he breathed in a stertorous voice. "I'm throwing my hat in the ring."

"But you don't have a hat," Dooley pointed out in an admirable display of logic.

"Look, fellas," Brutus heaved. "Look over there."

We looked over there, and that's when we saw what had suddenly made him pant like a pointer. It was Diego and Harriet, seated on the roof of The Hungry Pipe, the popular restaurant that's one of the marina's draws. I could just make out their silhouettes as they were sitting, heads together, backlit by that same moon that had fascinated Clarice so much.

"It's our spot," Brutus said, still sounding as if he'd swallowed a mosquito. "The spot I declared my everlasting love and devotion. The very spot I vowed to love and protect, to honor and cherish, to be all that I could be..." He heaved a soft sob, and for perhaps the first time since I'd made his acquaintance, I could see actual tears glisten in the tough cat's eye.

"That's not very nice," said Dooley, in a massive understatement.

"He's doing it on purpose," Brutus said. "He knows how much this place means to me and he's just rubbing my nose in it."

It seemed a little far-fetched to think that Diego would know when Brutus would pass by The Hungry Pipe and see him and Harriet on the roof. The cat might be evil, but he was not clairvoyant. What had probably happened was that Harriet must have pointed the spot out as one she favored, and Diego decided to humor her and see what the big deal was.

The big deal is that Colin Carret, the Pipe's proud owner and a perennial optimist, always overestimates the appeal of his place, and prepares more food than his clientele can ever tuck away. And since his kitchen happens to be on the top floor of the building, a lot of that food makes its way into his garbage bins, which are located on the roof before being transferred to the alley below via the kitchen elevator in the morning. Every cat in Hampton Cove knows that the Pipe is the place to be to get your paws on some high-quality grub.

I decided not to introduce this sordid materialistic theme into the conversation. Brutus was hit hard enough as it was. And as we watched, Diego and Harriet's profiles retreated, and moments later we could see them descend the fire escape, reach street level, and stalk off in the direction of home and hearth, where presumably Diego would eat my food, drink my water, poop in my litter box and take my place at Odelia's feet.

"I can't go home," Brutus announced brokenly, and staggered towards that same fire escape, and was soon mounting the steps, in the throes of a debilitating emotional crisis.

"We can't leave him like this," I told Dooley.

"Yeah, he doesn't look very happy," Dooley announced.

"You wouldn't be happy if you were forced to watch the cat you loved canoodle with some other cat."

"I've been watching Harriet canoodle with other cats all my life," Dooley reminded me. "I think I'm a canoodling expert by now—at least where it concerns Harriet."

He was right. Dooley had always nursed a quiet passion for Harriet—a passion which unfortunately had never been reciprocated by the haughty white Persian. "One day, Dooley," I told him. "One day you'll find the cat for you."

"I already found the cat for me. She just hasn't found me yet," he said simply.

I never knew my best friend was a closet philosopher, and the upshot was that as I trotted after Dooley, who was trotting after Brutus, I had to wipe a tear from my eye, too. It was that moon. It was having a strange effect on all cats—even hardened ones like me.

"When are you going to fall in love, Max?" asked Dooley as we mounted the stairs.

"I've had my brushes with romance," I told him.

"I know you've had your flings, Max, but when are you going to find true love?"

I shrugged. "I dunno, buddy. When true love finds me, I guess?"

"You are by far the most unromantic cat I've ever met."

"I simply don't like being tied down. I'm a free agent, Dooley."

"You just haven't found the right one yet, Max."

I didn't enjoy this conversation, so I decided to cut it short by ghosting my friend for the rest of the climb up the creaking, rusty contraption. The ladder was Colin's fire escape and rarely used by humans except for couples to sit and pucker their lips for a smoke or a kiss or both. For cats, though, it was the main gateway into Colin's culinary paradise, for it led straight to the spot on the roof where he liked to dump the Hungry Pipe's tasty leftovers.

The scent that drifted down was intoxicating, and as usual about half a dozen cats could be found snacking on the premium morsels. When they saw us, they turned their heads. All of them were in cat choir and had refused to choose our side in our enduring conflict with Diego. In return, we ignored them. I must admit cats aren't above being petty.

Brutus had dragged his weary bones to the spot where Diego and Harriet had been enjoying each other's company, and Dooley and I watched him with a measure of concern.

"You don't think he's going to jump, do you?" asked Dooley.

"Cats don't commit suicide," I told him. "Only humans do."

"And why do you think that is?"

"Because cats are too smart to hurl themselves off rooftops. Besides, we tend to land on our feet. And then there's that whole nine lives thing to consider. We'd have to plunge to our deaths nine times before the jig is up, and who wants to go to all that trouble?"

"Maybe we should tell Brutus before he takes the plunge," said Dooley.

"He'll be fine. And the moment we drive Diego out of town he'll be even better."

"You think we'll be able to drive Diego out of town?"

"We did it once, we can do it again," I said with a conviction I wasn't really feeling.

"Clarice did it once," he reminded me. "And she's refusing to do it twice."

"So we'll do it ourselves."

"But how?"

"We'll figure it out."

We sat in silence, keeping a keen eye on Brutus, who clearly wanted to be alone at this point, and might have sat there for all eternity, if not a disembodied voice behind us had piped up.

"You were right," the voice said.

When we turned, I saw that the disembodied voice belonged to Shanille. She looked as miserable as a cat can look without possessing the opposable thumbs to hold a liquor bottle.

"He kicked me out," Shanille announced. "Diego kicked me out of cat choir, can you believe it? My own choir. The one I started. And he goes and tells me that from now on he's the new conductor. Says I couldn't conduct my way out of a paper bag. Basically calls me a talentless hack and a fraud. And the worst thing is that not a single member opposed him when he put it to a vote."

"I told you. He's pure evil," I said. Though I should have felt sorry for her, the fact that she'd thrown us out on our ears still rankled.

"I'm so sorry, Shanille," said Dooley commiseratingly. "I think you're a great conductor."

The tiger-striped tabby smiled weakly. "Thanks, Dooley. And I'm sorry for not listening to you before. You were right all along. I should have known better than to be taken in by his smooth-talking ways and his promises of endless supplies of Cat Snax."

"Those endless supplies of Cat Snax are paid for by Odelia," I told her. "Which makes him a liar *and* a thief."

"Oh, and to think my week started so great. Saw my favorite singer Charlie Dieber from up close—got a wink and a smile from him…" A beatific smile momentarily crept up her face at the sweet memory.

"Wait—you were there when the Dieber got shot?"

"Charlie didn't get shot," she said. "His bodyguard did."

A thrill of excitement rushed through me. "You saw what happened?"

"Of course I did. I saw the whole thing."

And she'd just finished telling us about her startling discovery when the sound of a human talking had me look up. Somehow the inflection sounded familiar, so I padded to the edge of the roof and looked down. "Hey, it's your human," I announced. Dooley joined me.

"Hey, it's Grandma," he said.

"That's what I just said."

Odelia's grandmother was walking down the street, in the middle of the night, talking on her phone for some reason. Odd. Very odd. Then again, this night had already proven to be the oddest night I'd had in a very long time. So Grandma Muffin roaming the streets of Hampton Cove at night was simply par for the course.

"Yes, Chancellor. No, Chancellor. Yes, Chancellor," she was saying, her voice carrying up to where Dooley and I were sitting and watching. "No, I don't think the current crisis can be solved with violence. Diplomacy is the solution, Chancellor Merkel. Oh, yes, I told Ban the same thing I'm telling you now. Yes, I will put in a good word for you. No big deal. Yes, I'm always at your service, Angela. Day or night. We all need to do what we can for world peace."

She passed around a corner and her voice drifted off.

"Angela Merkel," Dooley said musingly. "Somehow the name sounds familiar."

"German Chancellor. Top European politician. But why Grandma would be talking to her beats me."

"She's been talking to a lot of important people lately. She even talked to the President the other day."

"*Our* President?"

"I don't know. Do cats have a president?"

He raised an interesting question. Did cats have a president? I didn't think so. We're anarchists by nature, apt to adhere to no one. Then again, we do like Abraham Lincoln, since he allegedly used a golden fork to feed his son's tabby at White House dinners. I guess a guy like that is worthy of our everlasting allegiance.

Brutus seemed to have finally tired of sitting by himself, and wandered over. "You know? I'm starting to feel that maybe we should give Dieber a second shot at adopting us."

"He won't adopt us, Brutus," I told the cat, who'd clearly lost his mind. "We're males, and Charlie only adopts females."

"So what if I tell him I identify as female?" Brutus suggested. "Wouldn't that work?"

I wanted to ream him out for talking nonsense when there was a commotion behind us. The rickety fire escape was groaning and creaking violently, indicative of a large body climbing up. If this was a cat, it was a substantial one. Moments later, a head cleared the roof, and then a bare tattooed torso, and I saw that once again we were in the presence of Charlie Dieber.

"Hey, dudes and dudettes," the irrepressible singer caroled. "Now this is what I call a fine gathering!" He looked a little unsteady on his feet, swaying dangerously, his eyes half-lidded. I hoped he wouldn't come near the edge of the roof, for if he fell off and got squashed he wouldn't get up again. No nine lives for the Dieber. He caught sight of us and frowned, pointing a finger in our general direction. "Dudes! We have got to stop meeting like this!" He lurched, then pivoted, his arm outstretched, until he was pointing, like a weathervane, at Shanille. He blinked a few times. "Um, so are you a dude or a dudette, dude?"

"I'm a dudette, actually," said Shanille, whose exuberance had returned at the sight of her great idol.

"I think you're a babe," the Dieber announced, then did the most outrageous thing. He scooped Shanille up into his arms and started staggering back to the fire escape. "You've been adopted," he announced to a slightly startled Shanille.

"Oh, that's fine, Charlie," she trilled.

"Shanille!" I cried. "Where are you going?"

"Didn't you hear? I've been adopted by Charlie Dieber!"

"But... what about Father Reilly?" I asked, referring to her most recent human.

"He'll just have to learn to live without me," she said, and gave us a diva-like wave farewell. "Just like I'll have to live without cat choir! Goodbye, cruel world! Goodbye!"

The three of us watched, stunned, as Charlie disappeared down the fire escape, this time clutching the former cat choir conductor in his arms.

"I didn't know Shanille was such a drama queen," said Dooley.

"It would appear Diego brings out the worst in cats," I said.

"Charlie should have picked me," Brutus lamented. "I should have told him about my transition."

"Oh, stop talking nonsense, Brutus," I said. "Cats don't transition. Do they?"

"If it gets me out of the house I share with Harriet I'll do whatever it takes, Max. Anything is better than having to feel this pain. This searing heartache. This *tristesse*."

Wow. Talk about drama queens.

"It's the pain of lost love," Dooley said knowingly, then placed a sympathetic paw on Brutus's shoulder. "I feel your pain, brother Brutus."

"Sister," Brutus announced. "From now on I'm a dudette."

## CHAPTER 19

Odelia woke up from a loud noise. Since she'd spent half the night dealing with this Dieber knife business, it was a grumpy and decidedly annoyed Odelia Poole who opened first one tentative eye and then the other.

"What's with the racket?" she muttered, and discovered that the foot of the bed hadn't been slept on. "And where are my cats?" she added, suddenly thinking it ominous that neither Max nor Diego had come home that night.

Light was seeping through the curtains, and one intrepid sun ray had even had the gall of peeping through a split in the middle, where both curtains met, and was casting its bright and cheery light across Odelia's face.

"Ugh," she muttered, recoiling like a particularly timid vampire.

"Help!" a voice suddenly intruded her foggy thoughts. "Help me I'm stuck!"

Now she realized what noise had awakened her. It was Max, and he was in trouble!

"Max, I'm coming," she croaked. With an extreme effort she swung her feet from beneath the Garfield-motif comforter, inserted them into her pink Hello Kitty slippers, managed to rise from the bed without tottering to the floor, and shuffled out of the room.

"Somebody help me!" Max was yelling. "I know who did it!"

The introduction of this new theme threw her. Stuck, she understood. He must have tried to get in through the pet door and gotten stuck. But he knew who did it? Knew who did what?

She cursed herself for not leaving the kitchen door open last night—she'd been so beat that the moment she let herself into the house she'd staggered up the stairs, dropped into the bed and had been asleep in seconds, without giving a single thought to poor Max.

"I'm coming!" she repeated, picking her way down the narrow stairs. Even under normal circumstances it was a tricky staircase to negotiate, and in her current state of sleep deprivation it was a downright safety hazard. She managed to reach the ground floor unscathed and speed-shuffled into the kitchen, where she was greeted with a piteous sight: Max's head was inside the house, while the rest of his body was still outside.

"I can't move," he said when he caught sight of her. "I'm stuck, Odelia."

"Oh, poor baby," she said, kneeling down next to him. "I've asked my dad to fix this thing, and this time Chase is going to help him, so from now on you should be fine."

She placed her hands on his neck, and tried to ease him in.

"I don't think that's gonna work," Max said with a giggle. He'd always been ticklish.

"Just hang in there, baby. I'm going to get you out of this thing."

She decided to reverse her technique and shove him out

instead. So she pushed on his head, but that didn't work either. He was really and truly stuck. "Huh," she said, stumped.

She carefully opened the door and stepped out onto the paved deck, Max swinging with the door. Just as she'd surmised, the largest portion of the voluminous cat was sticking out, not unlike the iceberg that had sunk the Titanic. So now all she needed to do was get a firm grip on his body, and dislodge the rest of him.

"Can you breathe out for me?" she asked as she placed her hands on his trunk.

Max blew out a deep breath, she eased her fingers into his fur, and carefully pulled.

Dooley, who'd come walking up, stared at the scene. "This looks like a fun game," he said. "Can I play, too?"

"This isn't a game, Dooley," said Odelia. "Max is stuck."

"Oh." He thought about this for a moment. "Why?"

"Because Dad screwed up and made the pet door a size too small."

"Why did he do that?" asked Dooley.

"Can you stop asking stupid questions and just push my head?" Max burst out.

Dooley quickly trotted over. "Where do I push?"

"My head! Just push on my head while Odelia pulls my butt."

"Can't I pull your butt? I have a hunch I'd be great at butt-pulling."

"Just do it already!"

"Right," said Dooley dubiously. He clearly wasn't fully on board with the plan. He did as he was told, though, by placing both paws on Max's nose and pushing with all his might.

"Not the nose!" Max cried in a nasal tone.

Dooley, who was clearly not a professional cat pusher,

adjusted his position and placed his paws on the top of Max's head instead. The concerted effort of both cat and human finally yielded results, and soon Max popped from the pet door like a cork from a bottle. And as he sat on his haunches, panting slightly, he announced, "Have I got news for you, Odelia. Thank you, by the way, for getting me out of this hellhole."

"It's called a pet door, Max," said Dooley. "Not a hellhole."

Max gave his friend a dark look, then continued, "Oh, boy, did we have a night."

"A night to remember," said Dooley.

"Charlie Dieber tried to kidnap us, before his driver told him we were three males and then he kicked us out of his limo and into a ditch," he began.

"And then we saw Diego and Harriet on the rooftop of The Hungry Pipe and Brutus had a meltdown," Dooley added.

Max turned to him. "Are you going to tell the story, or am I?"

"You tell the story," Dooley said graciously.

"Then we saw Gran talking to Angela Merkel, and Shanille being sad because Diego took her place as cat choir conductor, and—"

"And then Charlie Dieber showed up again and adopted Shanille!" Dooley cried with a laugh. "What a night!" When Max shot him a glare, he added, "Sorry. Please continue."

Odelia frowned. "Grandma was talking to Angela Merkel? But why?"

"Giving her advice on world peace or something," said Max, waving an impatient paw. "The thing is, before she got adopted by Dieber, Shanille said something." He raised a whisker and paused for effect. "She was there when Dieber's bodyguard was shot."

"She saw who did it!" Dooley cried triumphantly.

"She saw who did it!" Max said, giving Dooley a nasty look. "It was—"

"—one of the other bodyguards!" Dooley caroled, at which point Max gave his shoulder a slap. Dooley returned the slap, and for a moment a lot of slapping ensued.

"Break it up, you guys," said Odelia. When Max and Dooley were staring up at her, panting slightly from the exertion, she asked, "Can you repeat that last thing?"

"One of the bodyguards killed the other bodyguard," said Max.

A trill of excitement shot through her. "Are you sure?"

"Yes, we are!" said Dooley. "Shanille is a big Dieber fan, so she had a front-row seat to his radio show thingy. She said one bodyguard approached the other bodyguard and spoke to him in a menacing tone of voice. There was some kind of scuffle and some shoving and then, suddenly, the bodyguard was shot! She saw everything because she was on the ground and had the dog perspective!"

"Frog perspective," Max corrected.

Dooley frowned. "Yeah, I don't get that."

Her heart bouncing against her breastbone, she crouched down and took Dooley's face in both hands. "This is very important, Dooley. What did the shooter look like?"

"Shanille didn't say," said Dooley.

"She did say he had the same color as me," Max said.

"Oh, that's right," said Dooley. "Orange."

"Blorange. I'm blorange. How many times do I have to repeat it?"

Just then, Brutus came trudging up, looking like something the cat dragged in. A different cat than himself, obviously, for cats can't drag themselves in. "Blorange is not even a color, Max."

"It is, too!" Max cried, cut to the quick.

In spite of her excitement about having solved the case—

or, rather, of Shanille, Max and Dooley having solved the case, Odelia couldn't help giving Brutus a worried look. "What happened to you, Brutus?"

"He broke his heart," said Dooley knowingly.

"I had my heart broken," Brutus corrected him.

"Oh. Diego and Harriet," she said, understanding dawning. "I'm so sorry, Brutus."

When you communicated with cats the way she did, you soon realized that their lives were a never-ending version of *The Bold and the Beautiful*. Or maybe even *The Young and the Restless*. Though neither soap opera could hold a candle to the drama cats could create.

"I'm going to put myself up for adoption," Brutus announced somberly.

"But you can't," said Odelia. "This is your home now, Brutus."

"I can't share a home with Harriet and Diego," said the cat morosely. "I'm going to elope to Charlie Dieber."

"Charlie doesn't adopt male cats, you know that, Brutus."

"He's going to have the transformation," said Dooley.

"Transition," Max corrected him.

Brutus gave her a wan smile. "From now on please call me Bruta."

CHAPTER 20

Odelia parked her pickup in front of Uncle Alec's house and got out. It was still early, and the street was pretty much deserted. But this couldn't wait. So she walked up to the house, which was a modest row house in a street of similar houses, and rang the bell.

It took a long time before there was movement inside, but finally a bedraggled-looking Chase opened the door. He was dressed in boxers and a flannel shirt that was open and displaying his chiseled chest and stomach. She gulped slightly and had a hard time dragging her eyes away from his washboard tummy and up to his face again.

He gave her a lopsided grin and rubbed the stubble on his chin. "Hey, Poole. I thought you said I had to bring a cannon to wake you? And look at you now, up and about."

"My cats woke me up," she said.

"Tough luck. So you decided that if you were up, I should be up, too?"

"I, um... had another hunch, Chase."

"Who is it?" a voice yelled in the background.

"It's your niece! She says she's got another hunch!"

Uncle Alec appeared, rubbing his eyes. He was also dressed in boxers and a checkered flannel shirt that was unbuttoned, only his revealed a sizable belly and a pair of impressive man boobs. "Odelia, honey, do you know what time it is?"

"No idea. All I know is that we need to go out to the Dieber place again. I think I know who did it."

Chase grinned. "Isn't she amazing? Keeps getting those hunches."

"Yeah, she is," said Uncle Alec, stifling a yawn. "So who did it?"

"Do you remember Toby Mulvaney? The red-headed guy?"

Chase frowned as he tried to recollect. "The security guy?"

"When Regan told us about her affair with Ray Cooper, she shot a quick glance at Mulvaney, and he looked away. I'll bet there's something going on between those two."

"You seem to forget that whoever shot Ray was actually going after Dieber."

"What if that's not the case? What if Ray Cooper was the real target?"

Chase gave this some thought, and finally Uncle Alec clapped him on the shoulder. "Listen to Odelia, Chase. She's always right."

Chase nodded slowly. "So we've been looking in the wrong direction all this time? Is that what you're saying?"

It wasn't what she was saying—it was what her cats were saying, but she nodded. "Maybe we should talk to Toby. I have a feeling he might be able to tell us something."

"You know what? Why don't the two of you go out there and talk to what's-his-face," said Uncle Alec. "While I go over to Odelia's and give Tex a hand with that pet door before he wrecks the damn thing."

Odelia gave her uncle a grateful look, and he returned it with a wink. Unlike Chase, Uncle Alec knew all about the Poole gift of being able to talk to felines. He'd told her many times he wished he shared her facility. But unfortunately only Poole women had the gene.

Chase held up his hand, fingers spread. "Five minutes. Quick shower and I'm all yours."

"All mine?" she asked with a cheeky grin.

He returned the grin, then pulled her in for a kiss. "All yours," he repeated.

"Oh, boy," said Uncle Alec, and watched Chase jog into the house, then up the stairs. Moments later, they could hear the shower running. "Max told you about Mulvaney?" he asked.

"He heard it from Shanille, Father Reilly's tabby? She was there when Ray Cooper was shot. Saw the whole thing. Said it looked like this Mulvaney guy was picking a fight with Cooper, getting into his face. Moments later the shot was fired and Cooper was dead."

"Those cats of yours are a godsend, Odelia. I just wish I could deputize them."

"If you want to see your face on the front page of the *National Enquirer* you should do just that," she said with a laugh.

"If they solved this case, I'm giving them a medal. I swear to God."

"And where are you going to pin it?"

He mussed up his hair. "Good question. Maybe I'll buy them a toy instead."

"Cat Snax. You can never go wrong with Cat Snax."

"Imagine paying your best detectives in cat kibble."

"Wouldn't that be something?"

"Easy on the police budget, too."

Chase came jogging down the stairs, now dressed in jeans

and a fresh shirt, and they were off. His hair was damp, a lock dangling across his brow, and he smelled of musk and cologne. As they climbed into her pickup, the heady scent of manliness made her swoon.

"Are you all right?" Chase asked. "You look kinda feverish."

She swallowed. "I'm fine." And so was he.

It didn't take her more than twenty minutes to make the drive to the Dieber place, and this time the guards greeted them like a couple of old friends. Inside, there was sheer pandemonium, as usual, only this time it wasn't because of Charlie's antics but because of a lack of Charlie.

"He didn't come home last night!" Roulston screamed. Now he was the one pacing the living room. "No telephone call, no messages, no nothing! We have no idea where he is! He took off last night—after you guys caught Luca—and hasn't been seen since!"

"He's probably still driving around," Odelia said. She told the security man about her run-in with Dieber. She also told him he'd been seen at The Hungry Pipe—though she refrained from mentioning the source of her information—and that another witness had told her Charlie was on some kind of crazy cat-collecting all-nighter.

Roulston dragged his hands across his stubbly head. "That kid is driving me nuts! Collecting cats, partying in the wake of an assassination attempt, leaving the safety of the compound to go on some joyride! He's every security professional's worst nightmare!"

"He's with his driver," I said. "I'm sure if you call him he'll be able to tell you where they are."

He walked off, taking out his phone and angrily jabbing it to life.

"How come you know so much about what the Dieber was up to last night?" asked Chase.

She gave him what she hoped was an enigmatic smile. "I have my sources."

"So you have," he said with a shake of the head.

They caught sight of Toby Mulvaney and joined him.

"Do you have a minute?" she asked the large red-headed man.

He gave her a curious look. "Sure. What do you want to know?"

They walked out of the living room, through sliding glass doors and onto the deck. The pool area was quiet this morning, Dieber's Bediebers probably still sleeping. Several cats stalked about, stropping themselves against the lounges, while others lay around, blinking at the morning sun and generally being their lazy, perfectly contented feline selves. Odelia counted at least a dozen, with more probably inside enjoying a hearty breakfast.

"The thing is, a witness has come forward," said Chase, once again lying his heart out. "This witness claims you got into a fight with Ray Cooper just before he got shot."

Toby laughed. "Me? Get into a fight with Ray? Better send your witness to an eye doctor. Ray and I got along great."

"Our witness is adamant, Toby," said Odelia. "She saw you and Ray. Up close."

Chase darted a curious look in her direction, and mouthed, 'She?'

She nodded and watched how Toby's face fell. "This witness, who is she?"

"We can't disclose her name," said Chase. "But she's ready to testify in court."

His jaw worked, but he wasn't talking. Odelia decided to try a different tack.

"Look, we know there's something going on between you and Regan, Toby. Were you jealous of Ray? Is that why you shot him?"

"Shoot him! I didn't shoot Ray. Did Regan tell you this? Is she the witness?" They merely stared at him, and finally he cracked. "Look, it's true that Regan and I—we had a thing going on, okay? But then she fell for Ray and things got kinda… complicated. She'd broken up with me but there were still all those feelings, you know? I wanted her back, and she wasn't sure which one of us to choose. And as long as I still had a shot—I mean," he quickly amended, "a chance of getting back together with her, I definitely wasn't saying no."

"So she basically had a relationship with both you and Ray?" asked Chase.

"Yeah, basically that's how it was. Now? I have no idea. She's still pretty busted up about Ray getting shot—which I had nothing to do with, by the way. I may have given him a piece of my mind that morning, and that may have looked like I was threatening him, but I sure as hell didn't shoot the guy."

"But you hated his guts."

"Yes, I did," he admitted. "Same way he hated mine."

"That must have been tough," Odelia said.

"It was a living hell to have to work so closely together with Regan and Ray."

"Can we take a look at your room?" asked Chase.

He emitted a hacking laugh. "Why? To find my gun? Go ahead. You won't find one."

"Because you got rid of it?"

"Because I never had it in the first place! I didn't kill Ray, Detective. I swear."

Just then, there was a commotion inside the house, and they all walked back in. To Odelia's surprise, Charlie Dieber had arrived, and he'd come bearing gifts in the form of three cats: Shanille, Diego and Harriet!

CHAPTER 21

Charlie held Shanille in one arm with Harriet in the other. His driver was left with the task of holding onto Diego, who, judging from his expression, had preferred to be in Shanille's place instead.

"Fresh felines! Three fine fresh felines!" Charlie was shouting, perhaps erroneously thinking he'd arrived at a farmers' market. "Fresh female felines for the Dieber collection!"

"Don't think this one's a female, boss," said the driver, darting an anxious glance at Diego. He clearly wasn't as big a fan of cats as his employer was.

"Nonsense!" cried Charlie, who was dressed in low-riding khaki cargo pants and nothing else. Odelia thought she preferred the star-spangled boxers. "Three fine babes for the Dieber!" Then his eye fell on Odelia and Chase. "Oh, hi," he said, stalking up. "Now aren't you a sight for sore eyes." He dropped the cats to the floor and held out his hand. "Charlie Dieber at your service, doll face. And aren't you the prettiest, hottest, sweetest piece of—"

"We met," Odelia cut him off. "Odelia Poole. I work with the police."

Charlie narrowed his eyes at her. "Oh, right! The cop chick. Now I remember."

"Hey," Chase said, stepping between Odelia and the pop star. "Show some respect."

The Dieber held up his hands in a defensive gesture. "I'm all about respect, dude. I respect the hell out of this hot piece of—"

"And for your information, those are my cats," said Odelia, pointing at Harriet and Diego. "You can't just steal people's cats. And that is Shanille. She belongs to Father Reilly."

He glanced down at Shanille. "Father Reilly, huh? I thought she looked a little austere. No ray of sunshine, that one."

"So if you don't mind, I'll take these back, and I will ask you not to steal any more of Hampton Cove's cats. You simply can't do this, Charlie," she said, really getting going now.

Charlie grinned at Chase. "She's one hot pistol, isn't she?"

Chase gave the singer a look that could kill. It didn't seem to affect the kid in the slightest.

"I told you, boss," the driver said. "You can't go around taking cats that don't belong to you." He allowed Diego to leap from his arms and carefully started to pick at the mass of orange hair stuck to his driver's costume. "Now look at that," he muttered with an expression of distaste. "I'm gonna need one of them rollers. One of them sticky things."

"Look, I'm on a mission from God," the Dieber explained.

Odelia, who was thinking hard about removing her Charlie Dieber Spotify selection from her phone and canceling her fan club enrollment, heaved a soft groan. "Oh, God."

"Exactly! I collect cats, feed them, nourish them, shower them with the Dieber's love and affection, and then I gift them to my Bediebers. Why do you think I've got so many cats? I'm grooming them! They're my gift to the world, babe! A blessing for everyone. Bediebers get to hold a little piece of the Dieber in their arms—something to show them my true appreciation. My cats find a wonderful home. And I get to spread sweetness and light!"

She folded her arms across her chest, giving him a stern look. "You're going to give all these cats away?"

"From the Lord through me and into the world. I bless—you bless—bless you."

"You're telling me you steal cats from all over the place and then you foist them on some unsuspecting preteens?! You steal my cats and treat them as hand-me-downs?!"

He rubbed his hairless chest and giggled. "I wouldn't put it that way, babe."

A red mist drew up in front of her eyes. "HOW WOULD YOU PUT IT, THEN?!"

Chase, who saw she was about to throttle the Dieber, pulled her aside. "Please don't kill him, babe," he said. "He's a moron. I know that. You know that. Heck, I think even he knows it. But if you kill him I'm gonna have to arrest you and that would break my heart."

The red mist evaporated. "Arresting me would break your heart?"

"It would. So please calm down. We've got a murder to solve, and you going off on the Dieber isn't helping."

She threw up her hands. "It's fine. It's just that... the gall of the guy!"

"I know, I know. Deep breaths, babe. Deep breaths."

"Aargh!"

"In. And out. That's it."

She took a steadying breath, fists planted on her hips. "Stealing my cats."

"Well, technically Diego is my cat, Shanille is Father Reilly's cat, and Harriet is your mother's pride and joy."

She turned, watching Charlie play with the latest additions to his cat menagerie. Harriet seemed to enjoy the attention, and so did Shanille. Diego? Not so much.

"Okay," she said, closing her eyes. "Let's pick up where we left off. Where's Toby?"

They walked out of the living room and onto the deck, but the thickset bodyguard was gone. They returned inside, and mounted the stairs, then set foot for Roulston's office, hoping to find Toby ensconced there. The only one present and accounted for was Roulston himself. He quirked an eyebrow at them. "You were right, Miss Poole. Turns out Charlie was having some fun last night, picking up cats left and right."

"Stealing cats, you mean," she said.

"Deep breaths," Chase whispered.

She sucked in a few more breaths.

"Any idea where we can find Toby?" asked Chase. "We need to ask him a couple questions."

Roulston heaved the sigh of a long-suffering security man. "What has he done?"

"He—" Odelia began, but Chase shut her up with a glance.

"We just need to have a word with him, if that's all right with you," he said.

"Last room on the right. And please tell him to get his act together."

"Why is that?" asked Odelia.

"He's been acting weird all morning. Cagey, if you know what I mean. And he and Regan aren't on speaking terms for whatever reason." He shook his head. "Place is falling apart.

Cat-napping pop stars, drama queen bodyguards, murder and mayhem…"

Odelia exchanged a look with Chase, and they went in search of Toby. They passed a room whose door was open and saw Regan lying on the bed, tossing a tennis ball at the wall and deftly catching it. She was frowning so hard and lost so deeply in thought she didn't even notice Chase and Odelia looking in on her.

"Last room on the right," Chase muttered. The door was closed, and he gave it a knock. Loud techno music was coming from inside the room, a pulsating beat that drowned out any other sound "Toby?!" he yelled. "We never finished that conversation, buddy!"

When no response came, except for the staccato thump of the speakers, he pushed down on the door handle. The door swung open, and the next moment Odelia clapped her hands over her mouth to stifle a scream.

There, on the floor of the small room, lay Toby Mulvaney, his eyes open and staring unseeingly up at them. In his hand, a small-caliber gun. And in his temple, a nice round hole.

CHAPTER 22

Brutus, Dooley and I were watching as Tex and Uncle Alec worked on the pet door. It was a fascinating sight. Like watching a train wreck in slow motion. The two men had had some trouble removing the door from its hinges, but had finally managed to place it on top of a workbench Tex had dragged over from his garden shed. They'd hemmed and hawed for a while, scratching their heads and trying to decide how to do this thing, and had then both decided to take a break and had gone inside for a cup of coffee and a chocolate donut.

When they came out again, the door was still there, the pet door was still too small, and so they went straight back to dilly-dallying and drawing up a plan of campaign.

They kept darting furtive glances in my direction, and at one point Tex came over with a tape measure, wrapped it around my belly, then returned to the door and scratched his head some more.

"He's measuring you for your coffin, Max," said Brutus, who'd become very morbid since he'd begun his transition into Bruna. "Soon they'll lay you to rest in the backyard."

Dooley's eyes went wide. "They're going to bury Max? But why? Are you sick, Max? Is there something you're not telling me?"

"I'm not sick, I'm not dying, and nobody is going to bury me," I assured him with a reproachful look at Brutus, who merely lifted his shoulders. "They're simply trying to make the pet door fit to my particular... size."

"Which is considerable," Brutus commented nastily.

"Which is normal for the type of cat I am," I corrected him haughtily.

"A fat cat."

"A big-boned cat. I simply share more of my DNA with the big cats of the jungle than most," I told him, reciting something I'd seen on the Discovery Channel. "Your tigers, your lions, your leopards, your jaguars..." I shrugged. "I guess you could say I'm part domestic cat, part member of the Panthera genus—the big cats that roam wild and free on the Serengeti."

Brutus rolled his eyes. He was clearly not in the mood for a lesson in biology. Dooley was staring at me, though, clearly impressed. "Wow, Max. I never knew you were a tiger."

"Yeah, well," I said, flicking a speck of sawdust from my fur. "Scientia potential est. Knowledge is power."

"Michael Jackson?"

"Francis Bacon."

"Is he the one who invented bacon and eggs?"

"He could very well be, Dooley. He could very well be."

Just then, Grandma came strolling through the hole in the hedge that divides our two gardens. She was frowning, and talking animatedly into her phone. "Of course, Mr. President. I know, Mr. President. You're absolutely right, Mr. President. Yes, I'll get on it right away, Mr. President. Yes, I agree with you that world peace is what we should all be striving for, but at what cost, Mr. President? At what cost?!"

She disappeared through the hedge again, and Uncle Alec directed a puzzled look at his brother-in-law. "Is she talking to the President?"

Tex sighed. "Yeah, looks like. I don't know what's gotten into her lately, but she's been consulting with world leaders all week. Some guy called Ban Ki-moon, the Pope, of course, and now the President... She even talked to Bill Gates the other day."

"But why? And how come they even listen to her?"

"Beats me, Alec. What I've learned over the years is to simply let Vesta be Vesta. If these world leaders want to take advice from your mother, they have my blessing."

"And mine," said Alec, looking slightly taken aback. It's not every day that your mother becomes the go-to person for the top leaders of the world.

Just then, my cat ears pricked up, and so did Dooley's and Brutus's. We exchanged a look of understanding, and simultaneously said, "Odelia!"

Then Brutus sniffed, and his face lit up. "And Harriet!"

Moments later, Odelia came walking through the kitchen door opening—now without door—and smiled when she saw her dad and uncle hard at work—or at least thinking hard about work. "Hey, you guys. Am I glad to see you."

In her arms she was holding Harriet, who meowed plaintively, and only relaxed when Odelia had placed her on the ground. Immediately Brutus ran up to her. "Harriet, I…"

She gave him a supercilious look. "Please don't talk to me, Brutus."

I would have told her it was Bruta now, but I had the impression Brutus had had another change of heart, and had decided to give Harriet another shot at breaking it.

"Where's Diego?" asked Brutus.

"At Charlie Dieber's house."

"What?!" Brutus cried. "But… how?"

Harriet, who looked troubled, shook her beautiful white fluffy head. "Charlie grabbed me and Diego off the street early this morning. Told us he was adopting us. We decided to play along—just for the fun of it. But then Odelia showed up and blew a gasket. She took me and Shanille and wanted to take Diego, too, but by then he'd disappeared."

"Disappeared," repeated Brutus, looking like a cat who's seen Jesus.

"Yeah. He told me he was going for a bite to eat—the Dieber offers a nice spread of cat treats—but when Odelia went looking he wasn't in the kitchen. He must have slunk off."

"Slunk off," Brutus said, rolling the words around his tongue with relish. "Gone."

Harriet cut him a nasty glance. "Don't say it as if it's the best thing that ever happened to you, Brutus. I like that cat. I miss him."

Brutus grinned. "Trust me, sugar plum. You're better off without him."

"I wouldn't be too sure about that. Diego knows how to treat a girl. He's... gentle."

Brutus's smile vanished. "Please don't tell me. I don't want to know."

"Oh, leave me alone," she said irritably, and stalked off in the direction of the hedge.

"I'm not leaving you, Harriet," said Brutus decidedly, as he trotted after her.

"Can't you see I'm in mourning?"

"*You're* in mourning? *I'm* in mourning!"

"I'm pining, Brutus. Pining for Diego."

"And I'm pining for you, sweetcheeks!"

We watched them disappear into the next garden, arguing all the while.

"Good news about the disappearance of Diego," Dooley said.

"Yeah, great news," I agreed. "Let's hope he stays away this time."

"Not so great, you guys," said Odelia, who'd been listening while her dad and uncle messed with the door.

"Diego vanishing into thin air is the best news I've ever heard," I told her decidedly.

"Not that. Another bodyguard died. Shot to death in his room. The bodyguard Shanille thought killed Ray Cooper. Looks like suicide but..." She grimaced. "I'm not sure."

"Oh," I said, my exuberance waning. Rejoicing in the face of tragedy just wasn't right. "You're right. That is pretty bad. So you think he didn't do it?"

"Like I said, I'm not sure. He told us he didn't kill Ray, and I actually believed him, so..." She frowned. "The thing is, he was involved with Regan. They both were, Ray and Toby. Like a love triangle thing? Chase believes in the suicide theory, though. He's closed the case."

She was talking more to herself than to us, I saw. Humans often do that. They talk to themselves on the street, in the shower, in the car, thinking nobody can hear them. It's a peculiar habit. Then again, I think we can all agree humans are a peculiar breed.

"You want us to talk to Shanille again?" I asked. "Dig a little deeper?"

She looked up. "Mh? Oh, no. That's not necessary. Before I dropped her off at Father Reilly's I asked her to repeat to me what she told you. She said she couldn't be sure Toby actually shot Ray. All she saw was this strange exchange between them—which is understandable in the context of a quarrel between two love rivals. Which reminds me..."

She took a small pill bottle from her pocket and popped

the top. I gave it a suspicious look. I don't like pills. They usually taste horrible and tend to give me a nasty rash.

"What is that, Odelia?" asked Dooley.

"Vitamins," she said as shook two sizable pills into the palm of her hand. "Now are you going to swallow them like big boys or do you want me to mix them into your food?"

"Vitamins?" asked Dooley. "What's a vitamins?"

"They're good for you," she said. "They will give you more energy."

"I've got plenty of energy," I told her. "I don't need vitamins."

"I think I'll take one," said Dooley. "I like energy. Energy is good."

She smiled and placed a pill on his raspy pink tongue. He squeezed his eyes shut and dry-swallowed it, then gave her a look of triumph. She patted his head. "Well done, Dooley. You're a real champ." Then she turned to me and held up the second pill. "Your turn, Max."

I made a face, and Dooley said, "Max likes to roam wild and free on the Serengeti. He probably doesn't need a vitamins."

"Vitamin," she corrected him. "Plural: vitamins. So you're a tiger now, huh, Max?"

"And he likes bacon," Dooley added.

She grinned. "A real tiger wouldn't mind swallowing down a little pill."

"Oh, all right," I muttered, and opened my mouth wide. The things I do for my human...

## CHAPTER 23

After Odelia had watched her father and her uncle Alec work on her kitchen door for a while, she felt compelled to remove herself from the scene. By then it was clear to her that her door was not going to survive the efforts of two men who gave the handymen of this world a bad name. They'd begun by shaving off a small sliver of door, in a bid to make the pet door fit Max's outsized frame. Happy with the result, they'd decided to remove another bit of door, and had soon become addicted to the process. Now, at last count, it would appear they were moving steadily through the door like a pair of beavers chewing down a tree. At the rate they were going, soon there would be nothing left but a pile of sawdust.

She couldn't watch anymore, and retreated to the house next door, entering the kitchen to find her mother baking a cake. Marge looked up when her daughter entered the house. Her button of a nose was covered in flour, and her hair was covered with a wrap.

"Oh, hey, honey. Did they finish your door already?"

"Oh, yes, they finished my door," she said with a hollow

laugh. "Finished it off. I just hope they won't start hacking away at the rest of the house as well. Cause if they do, I might be forced to move in with you." She sat musingly for a spell. "You know? I never realized the kind of damage termites could wreak on a fragile structure. Now I know. It's not pretty."

Her mother made a sympathetic noise. "Oh, honey. I should have told you that your father and my brother are the worst handymen in the world. Remember how they were going to build a treehouse? When the dust finally settled there was no tree house, and no tree, either. You should have hired a professional for that door. They would have installed that thing in a matter of minutes."

"You're telling me now? I'm bound to be homeless by the time they're through."

Marge brought a hand to her face to hide her mirth. "Oh, honey," she said.

"It would be funny," she agreed, "if it wasn't so sad."

"It's just a door. I'll tell Tex to buy you a new one, this time with a pet door pre-installed."

Odelia glanced at the cake batter. She could go for a piece. Pity it wouldn't be ready for another few hours. "And then there's that Dieber business," she continued her lament.

"Oh, that's right. What's going on with that?"

"Turns out they weren't after Charlie after all. Just a lovers' tiff gone horribly wrong. One of the female bodyguards was involved with two of the male bodyguards, and one of them killed the other one and then killed himself with the same gun that he used to kill his rival in love. Or at least that's what it looks like at this point."

Mom looked up sharply. "What it looks like? What do you mean?"

She threw up her hands. "You know how I get these hunches? Chase used to make fun of them, but they're very real. And not just when the cats tell me stuff either. I could have sworn that this Toby Mulvaney was telling the truth when he said he didn't do it. And we talked to Regan Lightbody as well—she's the woman both men were in love with—and she says neither Ray Cooper or Toby ever showed violent tendencies. She was deeply shocked that Toby would kill Ray. Said it was simply not in his nature to do such a thing."

"What does Chase think?"

"Chase is happy that the case is closed and he never has to set foot inside Dieber Castle ever again."

Her mother laughed. "Dieber Castle? Is that what they call it?"

"That's what Dieber calls it. Oh, Mom, you should see the guy. You wouldn't like him. He's this bratty, annoying, self-absorbed pop star. A kid, really. Worse than you can imagine. I think I'll never be able to listen to his music again without remembering what a pain he is."

"You have to separate the art from the artist, honey. I'll bet if you met movie stars you wouldn't be able to watch a single movie anymore. And the same goes for musicians."

"Oh, and I lost Diego," she said, deciding to pour her heart out now that she was going so well. "Dieber went on a catnapping rampage last night and I only managed to retrieve Harriet and Shanille."

Mom checked the recipe in the latest cookbook she'd bought and frowned. "So much sugar. That can't be right. Perhaps I'll use half." She glanced up. "Diego is not a very nice cat, honey. Maybe it's for the best that he's gone missing."

"But I can't just give him up. He belongs to Chase—Chase's mother, actually."

"So?"

"So Chase asked me to take care of him. I can't go losing

his cats, Mom. What kind of person loses another person's cat?"

"Not all cats are created equal, Odelia. And Diego is clearly not cut from the same cloth as the others. So I say good riddance, and if Chase doesn't like it—tough luck. He's the one who foisted his cat on you, so I can't imagine he cares either way."

Odelia placed her head on the kitchen counter, enjoying the coolness of the marble against her heated cheek. She had to admit she'd never liked Diego all that much, and apparently he'd been wreaking havoc on her menagerie, stirring up trouble between Harriet and the others, and pestering Max by stealing his food, his water, his litter box and even his space on the bed. She'd hoped the feud would be short-lived, like the one between Max and Brutus had been, but her mother was right. As cats went, Diego was not a very nice one.

"Too much butter," her mother was muttering. "Clogging up Tex's arteries is not what I promised him when we exchanged wedding vows. Who wrote this? A serial killer?"

Just then, Grandma walked in, her iPhone glued to her ear as usual. Ever since Dad had gifted her the phone, she'd become an iPhone addict, taking the thing to bed with her and even wondering if she could take it into the shower. "Yes, Mr. President. Oh, but of course, Mr. President. I couldn't agree more, Mr. President." She held her hand over the phone and said, as an aside, "It's the President."

"I thought as much," said Odelia, amused.

Grandma returned to her most important conversation. "You will have to sit down with him at some point, Mr. President," she said as she took a seat next to Odelia and settled in for the duration. "Yes, everybody will be there. The American President, the German Chancellor, the French President, the Chinese General Secretary, the British Prime

Minister, His Holiness Pope Francis, of course." She rattled off a long list of dignitaries and Odelia exchanged a puzzled look with her mother, who merely shrugged and frowned at her recipe some more.

"Is she really talking to the President?" Odelia whispered, not wanting to interrupt her grandmother's apparently important phone call.

"President Putin," Mom clarified. "She's been trying to reach him all morning, and she's finally succeeded."

"Putin? The Russian dude?"

"Yep. For some reason she was very anxious he be included in her list of acquaintances."

"But... why? What's going on?"

"I haven't got a clue, and neither has Tex," said her mother. "We're just happy she's found herself a hobby that doesn't involve bees or horny old goats or running up a huge credit card bill. Ever since Tex got her that phone and a great deal on a mobile phone plan, it's been pure bliss. We hardly see her anymore. Just drops by for breakfast, lunch and dinner and that's it." She put her index finger and thumb together. "Model citizen."

Odelia studied her grandmother, who was now exchanging pleasantries with Putin. If she was happy, and Mom and Dad were happy, what harm could it do? Probably none. Besides, she had other issues to tackle. Like what to do about Diego. And what to do about this Dieber business. Chase might be happy with the way the case had concluded, but she wasn't. Something wasn't right, and she couldn't walk away until she figured out what.

CHAPTER 24

Watching Tex and Alec at work proved a great soporific. Very soon my eyes closed, and after a while I was sound asleep, perched on the hot stone floor of the deck. I only woke up when something prodded my ribcage, and I made a valiant attempt to slap them away.

"Lemme... sleep," I muttered.

"Max!" a voice intruded on my peaceful slumber. "She's gone!"

"That's great," I said, smacking my lips and turning over to my other side. I wasn't done sleeping. Not by a mile.

"Max!" the voice insisted, and finally I opened my eyes to see who this horrible disturber of the peace could be. I was about to give him a piece of my mind when I found myself staring into Brutus's green eyes. Once upon a time those green eyes had haunted my nightmares, but that was before Diego had come to town, and our enmity had turned into an unexpected alliance over shared grievances. The enemy of an enemy is a friend and all that.

"Brutus?" I asked, instantly awake. It's one of my finer qualities. Us cats can be asleep one second and wide awake the next. And we don't even need liters of caffeine to accomplish this amazing feat. "What's wrong, buddy?"

"Harriet's gone, Max. Said she couldn't live without him."

"Without who?"

I should probably have said 'whom' but I didn't think Brutus would care.

"Diego, of course! She was pining for him and whining about him and finally she left."

"Where did she go?"

"Dieber's place, of course! Where Diego was last seen." He placed a pleading claw on my front leg. "We have to go after her. She's going to get herself in all kinds of trouble. That place is like the Bermuda Triangle for cats! Enter Dieber Castle and never be seen again!"

"No, it's not. Dieber collects cats and then he gives them away to deserving Bediebers. Odelia told me all about it. To the Dieber cats are like swag. He puts them in gift bags and hands them out like so many pieces of candy or keychains or beauty products."

"That's... sick, Max."

"Yeah, it's not very cat-friendly," I agreed.

Brutus's eyes had gone wide. "He's going to give Harriet away! To who-knows-who!"

"He can't. She's not his to give away," I pointed out. Deep down, though, I knew he was right. The moment the Dieber laid his hands on a pretty Persian like Harriet, he would probably give her away to his biggest fan, which might mean she could very well end up in war-torn Afghanistan, Somalia or Syria. The kid had fans all across the globe. And even though Harriet and I rarely saw eye to eye, I would hate for her to meet such a terrible fate.

I gave Dooley, who was snoring softly next to me, a prod in the ribs. He woke up with a start and a snuffle. "Who's your daddy now?" he mumbled, promptly opening his eyes.

"I don't want to know," I told him. "Harriet's gone, and if we don't get her back she'll be on a plane to Kabul, Mogadishu or possibly even Damascus before we know it."

He blinked a few times. "Kabul? What's a Kabul, Max?"

"It's a city, Dooley, and not one Harriet will enjoy. It's hot there, and not so safe."

"She's gone back to Dieber's place," Brutus explained urgently. "And we all know what happens to cats once they enter that compound. They vanish! Without a trace!"

"Oh, no," said Dooley, fully on board now, his brain firing on all cylinders—which was just the one, in his case, but he definitely made it count. "Max, we have to save her!"

Dooley, who was president of the Harriet Fan Club long before Brutus had entered the picture, seemed even more anxious than his rival in love.

"The problem is that she went there of her own volition," I said. "Which makes it hard to organize an extraction." I'd seen plenty of action movies where SEAL Team Six goes in to save some hapless civilian, only to discover that said civilian has sold our heroes down the river, to be faced with the drug kingpin's wrath until all that's left is SEAL Team Zero.

Dooley stared at me, wide-eyed. "You mean…"

"I mean that Harriet could very well sell us to the Dieber, and before we know it we'll be the ones stuck in Kabul, Mogadishu, Damascus or possibly even Kinshasa, Congo."

"I don't want to go to Congo, Max," Dooley intimated. "I'll bet they don't even have Cat Snax there."

"Who cares about Cat Snax?!" Brutus thundered. He'd been following the discussion with rising impatience. "We go in. We snatch Harriet. We get out. It's as simple as that."

"And what if she doesn't want to be snatched?" I asked. "We can't very well force her to leave with us, Brutus."

"We could sedate her," Dooley suggested. "Give her a shot

of some mysterious clear liquid that will knock her out until she's safe and sound back here. It's what Bruce would do."

"And where are you going to find this mysterious clear liquid?" I asked.

"Um…"

"Exactly."

"Look, you guys, we have to at least try," said Brutus. "She doesn't know what she's gotten herself into. This Diego character will prove her downfall, and I couldn't live with myself if I didn't know I'd done whatever it took to save her from a fate worse than death."

"What's a fate worse than death?" asked Dooley.

"Being shipped off to some rabid Bedieber, of course!" Brutus cried. "Now are you with me or not? If not, I'm going out there alone—do or die!"

"I'm with you, Brutus," said Dooley. "Though I'd rather do than die."

"Me, too," I said. "I'm a doer not a dier."

And so we touched paws on it. Mission Save Harriet was officially a go.

## CHAPTER 25

We were back at the Dieber compound, a place I thought I'd left in my rearview mirror. Then again, one has to put aside one's misgivings when one's friend is in grave danger. It may surprise you that cats, who have a reputation for being selfish and individualistic, would come to the aid of a friend. But if I didn't do this, I'd never hear the end of it from Brutus and Dooley, Harriet's biggest champions in the entire world.

And I had to admit I kinda liked the feisty Persian, too. She might be a pain in the patootie but she was also a dear friend. Even though her Diego fixation was exasperating.

The moment we were past the gate, we moved in single file, just in case the enemy was lying in wait, and kept our ears to the ground and our eyes peeled, so to speak.

"Enemy activity at our six," Brutus suddenly whispered.

"Six? What's our six?" asked Dooley.

"Our rear!" he hissed.

I looked over my shoulder while Dooley checked out his butt. A guard was having a smoke and taking a stroll in the garden. He didn't look particularly dangerous to cats.

"Another bogey at one o'clock!" Brutus warned.

"A booger?" asked Dooley.

"Not a booger! A bogey!"

"What's a bogey?"

"I have no idea, Dooley," I said. I did see a cat lying on his back on the lawn, four paws in the air, his mouth open and a trickle of drool on his fur, clearly enjoying the feel of the sun on his jelly belly. How Brutus would know that this cat's name was Bogey I did not know, nor did I care. All I cared about was making sure we weren't captured by the Dieber and shipped off to some godforsaken place to live with one of his crazed Bediebers, no Cat Snax in sight.

Brutus suddenly held up his paw, claws clenched into a fist. "Sitrep! Stat!"

"Please speak English, Brutus," I said. "I have no idea what you're saying."

"We need to draw up a plan of campaign. I suggest we split up. Max, you cover the left flank, Dooley draws a bead on the right flank, and I'll engage from the front. Oorah!"

And he charged ahead, leaving Dooley and me to stare after him in bewilderment.

"Um. What did he just say, Max?" asked Dooley.

"No idea, Dooley. Let's just go and find Harriet. That's what we're here for."

"I like that," he said gratefully.

At a slight distance we followed Brutus and soon found ourselves in the pool area again, which was where Dieber Babes liked to hang out—both the human variety and the feline. Today wasn't any different. Dozens of young women were frolicking around in the pool, the Dieber himself the center of attention as he plunged around on an inflatable turtle, and wherever I looked I saw cats taking it all in their stride. Guarding this scene of peculiar bliss were powerfully built men and women, their heads swiveling continuously, their eyes roving, and little plastic thingies plucked into their ears which from time to time they touched with their fingers, at which point they spoke a few words to themselves.

Like I said, humans never think other humans can see them talking to themselves, which is kinda cute, actually.

"I don't see her, Max," Dooley informed me. "I don't see Harriet."

"Neither do I, Dooley. She must be inside."

And we were stealthily moving towards the house when suddenly a familiar cat blocked our access. It was Diego, and if possible he looked even more obnoxious than usual.

"No pasarán, dudes," he was saying.

"We're not here for the pasaran," Dooley said. "We're here to find Harriet."

"Though while we're here we might sample some of your pasaran," I said. I rubbed my tummy. "I'm feeling a little peckish."

Diego grinned. "I should have remembered you two have the mental capacity of a common housefly. What I meant to say was: you shall not pass!"

"Ooh! I've seen that movie!" Dooley said excitedly. "Um... It's on the tip of my tongue. I want to say... *The Goonies*? No! *Gremlins*! It's *Gremlins*, right?! I like *Gremlins*."

A scowl marred Diego's features at this demonstration of *Game of Fortune*. "Idiots! What I'm trying to get through your thick skulls is that you can't go in!"

"Why? Is something burning?" I asked, genuinely surprised by this cat's insistence.

"I'm in charge here now!" he cried. "And I don't want you here! Capeesh?"

"Oh." I finally saw what he meant now.

"You're in charge now?" asked Dooley. "Charlie must like you a lot, Diego, to put you in charge of his house."

"Not in charge of the house, you dimwit," he snarled. "In

charge of the Dieber Babes. And I'm forbidding you access to the house. So you better get lost or else."

"Or else what?" asked Dooley, genuinely interested.

Diego held up a menacing paw, extending his nails. The scene reminded me of *Nightmare on Elm Street*, a movie I'd wanted to unsee ever since I watched it with Odelia. For some strange reason she loves horror movies. I most emphatically do not.

I gulped, and so did Dooley. Not only was there no pasaran in this house, there was no neighborliness either.

But just then, a second cat materialized from the relative obscurity inside and drew up next to Diego. It was Clarice. "Oh, why don't *you* get lost, Diego?" she asked irritably.

"*You* get lost," Diego growled, harping on his favorite theme. "Or I'll cut you."

It was not something anyone had ever said to Clarice, I imagined, and I could see her expression darken into a vicious scowl. The next moment, a regular catfight ensued, and soon fur was flying and shrieks of pain were sounding. Within seconds, Diego bolted off in the direction of the garden, leaving a few drops of blood and a nice pile of orange fur on the floor. Clarice, who sat casually licking her paws, said, "There's something you need to see."

"Oh, we saw it," I said, suddenly overwhelmed by an irrepressible sensation of unbridled joy and affection for this inimitable cat. "And we liked it. Didn't we, Dooley?"

"I saw—I liked," Dooley confirmed, a look of admiration on his furry face.

"Not that. Something else," Clarice said with a frown. "Come."

And come we did—into the house that was hitherto forbidden territory, and then up the stairs and down a long corridor.

"I thought you said you were through dealing with Diego?" I said.

"That was before he started throwing his weight around," Clarice said as she sashayed across a nice white high-pile carpet. I had to resist the powerful urge to dig my claws in and start kneading. We were on a mission to save Harriet. Base urges had to wait.

"Is he really in charge of the Dieber Babes now?" asked Dooley.

"Of course he isn't. He just wishes he was. That cat has the biggest Napoleon complex I've ever seen in any living being. It's pathetic, actually, and a little sad."

"Um, what's a Napoleon complex?" asked Dooley.

"You may have noticed that Diego is a pretty short cat. To compensate he likes to act tough and whip other cats into submission. But not me. Uh-uh. If he tries that crap again, I swear I'll slice him up so bad his own mother won't recognize him. Oh, here we are."

I gulped, and so did Dooley. I'd seen Clarice gobble up vicious rats whole without batting an eye. I did not want to be on her bad side. If Diego kept this up, he was a dead cat.

We'd arrived at one of the guest rooms, and Clarice jumped and grabbed the door handle with both paws. The handle twisted down under her weight and the door opened.

"Hey, that's a neat trick," said Dooley.

"Stick with me. I can teach you stuff," said Clarice, pushing the door open further.

The room was smaller than I would have imagined in a house this size, and pretty messy. Magazines were strewn around, and when I checked the titles I saw they were all either gun-or baseball-related. A large poster of Alex Rodriguez adorned the wall over the bed, and a sizable banner of the New York Yankees covered the opposite wall.

"Looks like whoever lives here likes baseball," I said. "And guns."

"Over here," said Clarice, and moved into a bathroom the size of a cubicle. Over the sink, the mirror was bedecked with pictures, and when I looked closer, I saw they all featured the same woman.

"She's one of Dieber's bodyguards," Clarice said. "Her name is Regan Lightbody."

"Looks like this guy is pretty obsessed with her," I said. And then my eye fell on a few more disturbing details. The pictures of two guys had been marked with big red Xs over their faces.

Clarice had followed my gaze, and said, "Ray Cooper and Toby Mulvaney. The two bodyguards that were shot." She raised a whisker when I stared at a message taped beneath the men's pictures. It read, 'If I can't have you—no one can!'

"What does it mean, Max?" asked Dooley, who'd just spotted the same message.

"It means that whoever lives in this room is a double murderer," I said.

CHAPTER 26

It is always a tough proposition to be faced with two incompatible tasks. On the one hand I wanted to run and tell Odelia what we'd just discovered, so she could induce Chase to apprehend the killer. On the other hand, we'd arrived at the Dieber house with a job to do, namely to save Harriet from the cat-collecting and cat-distributing singer. And since I couldn't be in two places at the same time, I had a decision to make, and a tough one to boot.

Luckily I was helped in my decision-making process by the arrival on the scene of the very cat we'd come here to save: Harriet walked into the room and gave the three of us a vicious glare.

"Did you or did you not just attack my boyfriend?" she demanded.

I had the impression she was talking to Clarice, and that impression was confirmed when Clarice replied, "If you're talking about that obnoxious fleabag that calls himself Diego then yes, I did give him a piece of my mind. And if he wants more, he knows where to get it."

A challenging statement, but then Clarice had the chops to back it up.

"I'll have you know I lodged a formal complaint with the other Dieber Babes. They'll want to have a word with you. You can't go around cutting up cats, Clarice. You simply can't!"

"I can and I will if a cat gives me as much grief as your Diego does," said Clarice.

"Diego is the sweetest, most charming cat for miles around," she challenged.

"You're deluded if you think that cat's charming, honey," said Clarice.

But Harriet raised her chin. "Diego is a sweetheart, and I'll bet that the only reason you attacked him is because he rejected you. Diego is mine, Clarice, and you have no business trying to seduce him."

For a moment I thought Clarice was about to attack Harriet, for these were fighting words. Instead, she laughed —perhaps the first time I'd heard her utter such a musical laugh of genuine merriment. She laughed and laughed until tears rolled down her cheeks. Harriet's eyes, meanwhile, were shooting sheets of flame. Not that it affected Clarice in the least.

"Oh, you're funny, girl," said Clarice finally. "Me and that scuzzball. You wish."

"What's so funny about that? I know you tried to seduce him. He told me so himself. And when he said no, you attacked him. Poor cat said he never saw it coming. Lost a great deal of fur and I'm not sure those scratches on his nose won't leave a few very nasty scars."

"I hope they do," Clarice said. "The cat is a liar, Harriet. A big, fat liar."

"She's right," I said. "Diego threatened to cut Clarice, so she cut him. That's what happened. Isn't that right, Dooley?"

"That's exactly what happened," Dooley was happy to confirm. "Diego said, 'Get lost, Clarice, or I'll cut you.' Those were his exact words. He's not a very nice cat. Not nice at all."

"*You're* the liars!" Harriet cried, stomping her paw for good measure. "*You're* the big, fat liars! All of you. You, Max, are jealous of Diego because he's a much better singer than you and because Odelia likes him best. And you, Dooley, are jealous because I'm with Diego now and that drives you crazy, just like it drives Brutus crazy. And you, Clarice, can't stand it when a cat as attractive and charming as Diego prefers to be with me and not you. You're all jealous and you're all horrible, horrible cats and I never want to see you again for as long as I live!" And with these words, she took her leave, sweeping from the room like a diva.

"But Harriet!" Dooley cried.

She turned at the door, held up her paw and snapped, "Talk to the paw, Dooley!"

And then she was gone.

"Talk to the paw?" Dooley asked. "Why do I have to talk to her paw?"

"It's an expression," I said. "It means she doesn't want to listen to you."

"Oh, I'm used to that," said Dooley. "I just didn't see what her paw had to do with anything."

"Oh, Dooley, Dooley," said Clarice. "You are a sweetheart, aren't you? Let me just say it's her loss if she chooses Diego over you. The cat is a moron, and I don't say that lightly."

"Harriet is not a moron," said Dooley, coming to Harriet's defense even under these circumstances. "She just has a strange taste in cats, I guess."

"That's an understatement," I said.

And just as we were about to walk out and return home,

Brutus sailed into the room, moving at sixty miles an hour. "Where is she? I heard her voice! Where is Harriet?!"

"Tough luck, macho," said Clarice. "Harriet and Diego are back together and she'll scratch out the eyes of anyone who dares to come between them." She shook her head. "That's it," she announced. "This is the straw that broke the camel's back. I'm out."

"But you're not a camel, Clarice," said Dooley. "Are you?"

She smiled and gave his cheek a tender stroke—no claws involved. "See you around, Dooley. And you, Max and Brutus. And if you see Diego, kick him in the rear from me, will you? Don't hold back." She held up her paw and dropped something. "Clarice out."

After she'd stalked from the room, tail held high and head up, we stared at the item she'd dropped. It was a piece of Diego's fur that must have gotten stuck in her claws.

"What a cat," said Dooley admiringly. "What. A. Cat."

"Is it true what she said about Harriet?" asked Brutus, a pained expression on his face. "Is she back together with Diego?"

"Yes, it's true," I said. "She was in here ready to pick a fight with Clarice over Diego, accusing her of trying to steal him from her. Nonsense, of course, but Harriet bought it."

Brutus plunked down on his haunches, a haunted look in his eyes. "That's it. I'm out, too. This is the end, you guys. I'm done fighting."

"Good," I said.

"Why is that good?"

"Because we've got something to show you," I said, and led him into the bathroom.

CHAPTER 27

It was late in the afternoon when Odelia pulled up to the arts center in downtown Hampton Cove. The Seabreeze Music Center was usually reserved for local artists showcasing their talents, the occasional concert, ballet or musical performance, but today hosted perhaps the biggest star of the moment. Charlie Dieber was preparing to go on tour again, to promote his upcoming album, and had picked the Seabreeze for a tryout slash surprise gig. The venue chosen, he'd dropped clues on his social media accounts, and W-AWOL5 had also been spreading the word in the days since his appearance on their show.

When Odelia learned about the show from her uncle Alec, a tightness had spread across her chest, and she knew she had to be there to ward off whatever that little voice inside her head kept telling her. Not that the little voice was particularly intelligible, or even made any sense to her, but she knew something was wrong, and she had to try and stop it.

So she'd called Chase, who agreed to meet her at the

Seabreeze, and now she stood scuffing her toe on the pavement and biting her lip as she waited for the cop to show up.

Dozens of highly excitable girls stood giggling and gibbering animatedly, all wearing Charlie Dieber T-shirts, Charlie Dieber caps and some of them even sporting Charlie Dieber temp tattoos on their cheeks. One girl, who couldn't have been older than twelve, started singing 'Will You Love Me Forever?' and the rest quickly chimed in. It was one of Charlie's biggest hits, but for some reason it annoyed the heck out of Odelia now. She'd been such a big fan, but since she'd taken a peek behind the curtain and gotten a good look at the kid hiding there, she'd lost all respect. She felt like Dorothy, only Charlie was even worse than the Wizard.

Chase arrived and darted a curious glance at the dozens of kids now singing another Dieber hit. 'I want to be your boyfriend, will you be my girlfriend, baby?' they were yelling.

"I knew you were a fan, babe. I just didn't know you were such a big fan," Chase said with a grin. "Are you sure this is your crowd? You seem kinda old to be a Bedieber."

"Ha ha. Very funny. We're here on official police business, Chase. Not as fans."

"Official police business, huh? And you're not even a cop."

"You're the cop. I'm just here to make sure you arrest the right people."

Uncle Alec also joined them, looking slightly out of breath. "Damn. I had to park a mile away. This Dieber kid is popular."

"You figured that out now?" asked Chase, clapping his superior officer on the back.

"Yeah, I had no idea," Alec said, extracting a big white handkerchief from his pants pocket and wiping his brow. "Now what's all this about a security threat?" he asked.

"I don't think Toby committed suicide," Odelia said.

"You told me already. And I'm telling you he did.

Gunpowder residue on his hand, position of the body, fingerprints on the gun. He did it, Odelia. He killed Ray Cooper and then he killed himself when he realized you were onto him and he wasn't getting away with it."

She was shaking her head. "I don't buy it. I just…"

Chase and her uncle exchanged a glance. "Those hunches again, huh?" asked Alec.

"I thought you told Chase I was always right?"

"Yeah, but that was before you decided to ignore solid evidence. Did, um…"

"Did what?"

He darted a quick look at Chase. "Did one of your informants tell you something?"

"No. Not this time. This time I'm trusting my own gut."

This didn't seem to inspire her uncle with a great deal of confidence. If her cats gave her inside information from the feline world, he was fully on board. Now? Not so much.

But finally he shrugged. "You know? I've never been to a Dieber concert before." He frowned at the braying crowd of teenagers. "I'll bet it's a once-in-a-lifetime experience."

"Look at it this way, Chief," said Chase. "It'll help you stay young."

"Or deaf," he grumbled as he covered his ears.

The doors to the center opened, and the braying intensified, turning into a roar. As one girl, the troupe stormed the door, and practically flattened the man who'd opened it.

Once inside, Odelia was surprised to find the theater as big as it was. It had been ages since she'd been in here, last time for a Christmas show, and she hardly remembered.

They walked on through to the front, and proceeded to climb up to the stage, which was loaded with equipment ranging from guitars, synths, drum set, amplifiers, and even a baby grand piano, where, presumably, Dieber would play 'Girlfriend,' his breakthrough hit.

They were met backstage by Carlos Roulston, who gave them a curious look.

"When I got your phone call I honestly thought it was a prank," he said.

"Better safe than sorry," said Chief Alec.

"So there's been a threat? Is it credible?"

"Very credible," said Chase as he shot a look at Odelia.

Roulston nodded. "I hired some extra people so we should have everything covered. Appreciate the heads-up. Let's just hope your source was wrong and things go smoothly."

He walked off, barking some orders into his phone, and Odelia, Chase and her uncle watched from the wings as people milled about, and the theater quickly filled up.

"Looks like a full house," Chase commented. "The kid's a real draw."

"Did this 'hunch' of yours tell you where the threat will be coming from?" asked Uncle Alec, who appeared very unhappy to be there. He truly wasn't a pop concert fan.

"Not exactly," she admitted. "I just…"

"Have a feeling," he completed the sentence. "At least tell us if Dieber is the target."

"I don't know," she said helplessly. "Him or someone in his entourage."

"Right," said Uncle Alec dubiously. "Look, I need a smoke. Be right back."

"I didn't know he started smoking again," she said as she watched her uncle's retreating broad back.

"He smoked before?"

"Oh, yes. After Aunt Ginny died he started smoking like a chimney. My mom finally convinced him to quit. Dad helped by showing him some X-rays of lung cancer patients."

"He's not a big smoker. A couple of cigarettes a day. At least he doesn't smoke in the house."

"How's that working out for you, living with Alec?"

"It's great. We're like a comedy duo."

She smiled. "So who's Lucy and who's Desi?"

Chase grinned. "I'm definitely not Lucy, I can tell you that."

Uncle Alec returned, reeking of cigarettes, and announced, "Look who I found lurking outside the stage door." He stepped aside to reveal Max, Dooley and Brutus.

"Odelia!" Max announced urgently. "You have to stop him! He's going to kill her!"

She clamped her teeth together and crouched down. "Who?" she whispered.

"Nugent!" he cried. "I finally figured it out! Nugent is going to kill Regan!"

CHAPTER 28

Unfortunately, just at that moment Charlie Dieber walked onstage, to the booming roar of an ecstatic crowd, and the concert started. Whatever else Max was saying was lost on Odelia, for try as he might, he couldn't raise his voice over the racket.

The terrific noise caused Brutus and Dooley to hug the floor, trying to cover their ears, and Odelia searched around to see if she could catch a glimpse of Jason Nugent. But wherever the guard was, he wasn't here, and for a moment she feared he might already have struck. But then she caught a glimpse of Regan Lightbody, on the other side of the stage. She was keeping a close eye on the proceedings, her keen gaze swiveling from Dieber, as he performed, to the crowd. More guards had been placed in front of the stage, and they had a hard time preventing crazed teens, eyes wet with tears and screaming their lungs out, from trying to mount the stage and jump Dieber. Panties and bras and other items of underwear were being pelted onstage, along with teddy bears and lots and lots of plush cats.

Charlie took it all in stride, as he belted out his biggest

hits. He seemed in his element, and Odelia had to admit he looked really cool, and his voice sounded great, too.

And then she returned her gaze to Regan and saw to her horror that a man was sneaking up on her from behind, holding a large knife that flashed in the stage spotlights. She recognized the man as Jason Nugent. Chase had seen the same thing, and so had Uncle Alec. Ignoring the confused looks from Charlie and the members of his band, she wasted no time darting across the stage, yelling, "Regan! Regan, watch out—behind you!"

Regan saw her coming, and frowned, instinctively going for her gun. Then, when she saw Odelia pointing, she whirled around and saw the threat. Nugent, not expecting this, tried to plunge the knife into her neck, but she managed to ward off the blow with a slashing movement of her arm, causing her gun to drop to the floor. In response, the flat-nosed bodyguard dropped the knife and brought out a handgun of his own, training it on Regan.

Chase and Uncle Alec, who'd joined them, stopped short when they caught sight of the weapon, and held their hands up in a bid to put the guard at ease and stop the attack.

The concert, still in full swing, drowned out any words that were spoken, but the look on Nugent's face spoke volumes. For some reason Odelia didn't comprehend, he wanted Regan dead. Presumably he'd meant for the attack to look like another botched assassination attempt on Dieber, and if Max hadn't warned Odelia he might have gotten away with it, too. He still might, for he was cocking the gun now, Regan making pleading gestures.

Nugent brought his left hand up to steady his right, and took a two-handed stance, as if he was at the gun range, aiming his weapon squarely on Regan. He yelled something, then, which sounded a lot like, "If I can't have you, no one can!" but Odelia couldn't be sure.

"No!" she screamed, but knew it was too late. The man would fire and kill Regan.

And just when she was contemplating throwing herself on top of Nugent, help suddenly descended from the skies. Three cats dropped down, claws out. Max landed on the man's face, blocking his view, while Brutus dropped on his hands, knocking them down and causing the shot that he squeezed off to drill a hole in the stage floor. Dooley, unfortunately, missed his approach and landed on top of Uncle Alec's head, who quickly shook him off.

Max must have really dug in, for Nugent now dropped his gun, and tried to pry the outsized orange cat from his face. Like an alien facehugger, though, Max wasn't budging, and hung on tight. Odelia, who didn't want Max to suffer any harm, quickly came to his aid. It was hard to know what to do, though, for Nugent was lashing out all around himself, clearly crazed. Max was finally sent flying, and Odelia saw that the man's already damaged visage had been upgraded with a nice set of bloodied new scratch marks. Instead of one sliced eyebrow, he now had two. Too late, she saw that Nugent made a dive for his gun.

Sadly for him he met Chase's fist on his way down. The hit to the temple he sustained was so considerable that he was knocked back, and landed on the floor, out for the count.

The band, who'd finally realized something was amiss, had stopped playing. Not Charlie, though, who had his eyes closed and just kept on singing. Without the support of his musicians and especially his backing track, it soon became clear that Charlie Dieber's voice was weak, thin and flat at best. Even the assistance of voice amplification couldn't induce it to rise above a sad whisper. It soon became obvious to one and all: the kid couldn't sing!

There was a shocked silence in the crowd, but then people started booing and laughing. Dieber, opening his eyes and realizing he was singing all by himself, immediately stopped and held up a hand, displayed a wide smile and shouted, "I love you! Love you all!"

And then he fled the stage and disappeared into the bowels of the theater.

CHAPTER 29

They were in Dieber's dressing room, Odelia, Chase, and Roulston's crew. Uncle Alec had arrested Jason Nugent and taken him into police custody. Regan Lightbody, meanwhile, had a hard time coming to grips with what had just happened. Her tough demeanor had crumpled, and her face was tear-stained. She wiped her cheeks with the back of her sleeve.

"I knew he liked me. I just didn't know he was obsessed with me," she told Odelia.

Dieber had hit the shower and returned now, dressed in sweatpants and a hoodie. The concert, after hitting that unfortunate snag, had soon started up again, and since Charlie acted as if nothing had happened, soon his Bediebers had put the vocal mishap out of their minds as a one-time anomaly in an otherwise super show, and had resumed screaming.

"Great show," Charlie was saying to no one in particular. He sank down onto a couch and closed his eyes. "Best show ever, dudes."

"Is it true that Nugent shot Ray and Toby?" asked Regan, hugging herself.

"Yes, it's true," said Odelia. "He figured that if he could just get rid of them, you might turn to him as the next best thing. When that didn't happen, he decided to kill you, too, and make it look like someone was coming after Charlie and you got in the way."

"I never saw him that way. I considered him a friend. A colleague. Nothing more."

Roulston wrapped her into an embrace, and Odelia turned to Chase, who was shaking his head. "How the hell did you know?" he asked. "And how the hell did your cats save Regan? I just don't get it."

She smiled. "They must have crawled up into the stage rafters when they realized what was happening, and decided to jump on top of Nugent to try and stop him."

"Those cats of yours are something else, Odelia, let me tell you that."

"Yes, they are."

"And your hunches? I'm never making fun of you again. Ever."

"I'll hold you to that."

"Oh, please do. I mean, you should have been a cop, babe. You're aces."

"Thanks," she said, greatly touched. "I'm just glad we managed to save Regan."

There was a commotion at the door, and a girl burst in, followed by a woman with a clipboard and headphones. The girl was blushing and giggling and grinning like crazy the moment she caught sight of Charlie.

"Hey, Bedieber!" he said, getting up. "Come on in. Have I got a surprise for you!"

The girl proceeded into the dressing room. She looked all

of thirteen years old and was dressed in a Dieber tank top, pink bra, ultra-short skirt and not much more.

"If I were that girl's mother…" Odelia muttered.

"Yeah, but you're not," Chase said. "So shush, Poole."

She grumbled something as she watched the same assistant who'd ushered the girl in hand Dieber a large box. When he opened the box, she saw to her surprise that it contained none other than… Diego! The cat looked a little annoyed at having been stuck inside a box.

"Isn't that my mother's cat?" asked Chase, sounding as surprised as she was.

"It is."

"Do you like cats?" Dieber asked the girl, who nodded eagerly, her cheeks flushed.

"I love cats!" she squeaked. All that screaming had clearly affected her vocal cords.

"Here you go," said the singer, and handed her Diego. "Take good care of him."

"Oh, I will, Charlie!" she squealed, eagerly grabbing the cat. "I'll love him and cherish him and keep him forever! I'll feed him the best food and give him cuddles and huggies all day long!"

Odelia studied the girl for a moment. "Do you really like cats?"

"Oh, do I? I love cats! We've got twelve of them at the mansion."

"The mansion?"

"My father is the owner of Feline's Gold. My family lives in Southampton."

"Feline's Gold? The cat food company? The one that produces Cat Snax?"

She nodded enthusiastically. "I love cats. Almost as much as I love Charlie."

Diego gave Odelia a wink and a grin. "Sorry to leave you, babe, but looks like I just found myself a better deal."

"Now wait a minute," Chase said, stepping forward.

"It's all right, Chase," said Odelia, placing a hand on his arm.

He frowned. "But that's Diego."

"I'm sure he'll be very happy with this girl," she said. "What's your name, honey?"

"Kitty Nala."

"I'm sure Diego will be very happy with Kitty Nala."

Diego was still grinning. "Keep that hairy ape away from me, Odelia. I just hit the jackpot! Woo-hoo!"

Odelia leaned in, and whispered into his ear, "See you around, Diego."

"Fat chance," he replied. "I'm heading for cat paradise, babes! Adios!"

She stepped back, also smiling, and waved as Kitty Nala left the dressing room with Diego clutched in her arms. Some problems have a way of taking care of themselves, she thought. And this was one problem she was glad she didn't have to solve.

Dieber's assistant walked up again and delivered a second box to the singer.

"I want to give you a small token of my appreciation," he said, fixing Odelia with a sultry stare. "Turns out you saved the day. And even though they weren't trying to kill me—which came as a great surprise, and a slight disappointment—I still want to thank you."

"That's all right," she said. "Just doing my duty."

Chase leaned in, and whispered, "You even sound like a cop."

"Here," said Charlie, handing her the big box. "From me to you, babe."

She opened the box and to her surprise found Harriet staring up at her piteously.

The Persian gave a pleading little mewl, then said, "Please take me home, Odelia."

Odelia placed the box on the floor and pressed her lips together, fury lancing through her. "Charlie Dieber! You can't gift me a cat that you stole from me in the first place!"

"Oh, dear," said the pop star, closing his eyes. "Here we go again."

"This is Harriet! This is my cat!"

"How am I supposed to know who belongs to who?" the star asked with a shrug.

"You're the worst cat person I've ever met in my entire life!" she screamed, her cheeks reddening and her fists clenching and unclenching. "And you're a lousy singer!"

"Hey, now don't you go and get personal," he said, darting worried glances at her fists. He then directed a beseeching look at Chase, hoping the large cop would intervene, just like he had the last time Odelia had flown off the handle. But Chase merely smiled and folded his arms across his chest, clearly prepared to sit this one out.

"If you steal one more cat!" she shouted, wagging a finger in the kid's face. "One more cat, I swear to God!"

"Okay, all right! Jeezus. What's with you and cats? They're just a bunch of stupid animals."

She hauled off and slapped the singer so hard across the cheek the sound echoed around the dressing room. Charlie's personal assistant was there, Roulston was there, and so were Regan and the rest of the security guards. None of them interfered when Odelia gave the spoiled brat a slap across the face that he would remember for a long time to come.

"She hit me!" he cried, touching his cheek. "Do something! Arrest her! She *hit* me!"

But instead of arresting her, they all smiled and then

walked out. On his way out, Roulston leaned into Odelia and murmured, "Been wanting to do that for a *very* long time."

Odelia picked up her cat and, after firing off a look that could kill and making the singer wilt, she walked out. To her great satisfaction the imprint of her hand was nicely outlined on Charlie's face. A small gift from her to him. A token of her lack of appreciation.

EPILOGUE

After the crazy week we'd had, it was great to see things finally return to normal. To celebrate the conclusion of the Charlie Dieber case—although in actual fact it had turned out to be the Regan Lightbody case, and Charlie Dieber didn't feature into the affair at all, much to the singer's dismay—Tex decided to organize one of his fabled barbecues, and so the whole family gathered in Tex and Marge's backyard that night, to enjoy a nice dinner.

Brutus, Dooley and I had taken up our usual perch on the porch swing, where we had an excellent overview of the proceedings, and Odelia had set out some delicious treats for us—the same meat the humans snacked on, only ours was fully raw, of course.

Why humans want to ruin their food by cooking it is beyond me. Then again, a lot of the things humans do is a cause for head-scratching. Though I usually try not to let the revolting scent of their cooking or grilling interfere with my own enjoyment of the feast.

Harriet, who'd been in seclusion inside the house, finally walked out and joined us.

At first things were a little awkward between us. The last words she'd spoken still rankled. 'I never want to see you again for as long as I live' is one of those statements it's a little hard to walk back on. She was still alive, and she was seeing us right now, so…

She cleared her throat. "Look, you guys. I owe you an apology. I mean…" She cast an apologetic look at Brutus, her former boyfriend. "I guess Diego fooled me."

"Not for the first time," Brutus couldn't help but point out.

I placed a paw on his leg. "Don't be petty, Brutus. Let's hear what she has to say."

"Yeah, the joke is on me, isn't it?" Harriet said bitterly. "Fool me once, shame on you. Fool me twice…" She sighed, directing a searching look into the distance, beyond the cloud of thick, black smoke wafting up from Tex's barbecue, a clear indication he was torching his sausages again. "I thought he'd changed his ways, you know," she said. "He told me he was now a different, better cat. That I brought out the best in him. I guess Diego's best was not all that good to begin with. When I heard how happy he was to go and live with that Kitty Nala person, and that he didn't even give a single thought to me—as if I didn't even exist…"

She brought a distraught paw to her quivering lip, and tears glistened in her eyes.

It was obvious that she hadn't fully recovered from the terrible episode yet.

"I heard everything, you know. I was in my box but I could hear the whole thing."

"Oh, sweetness," said Brutus, sidling closer to her. "Forget about that cat. He isn't worth a single tear."

"I know," she said, nodding hard, then turned her tear-streaked face up to Brutus. "You're so nice to me, Brutus. Why are you so nice?"

"Because I care about you, babycheeks. You're my girl. You'll always be my girl."

"Oh, Brutus."

"There, there. Now lemme dry those tears. Everything is gonna be all right."

"Oh, honey bucket. I missed you."

"I missed you too, buttercup."

"Oh, booksie-bug."

"Oh, snooksie-tootsie-wootsie."

"I'm gonna be sick," Dooley announced, making a face.

I grinned. "Looks like things are back to normal on the home front, buddy."

"Yuck."

And while the lovebirds renewed their lovebirdiness, Dooley and I watched the Pooles come together and prepare to be poisoned by Tex's nonexistent barbecue skills.

"So did you get a confession, Uncle Alec?" Odelia was asking as she held up her glass of rosé.

"I most certainly did," the Chief said. "And I didn't even have to beat him up." When his comment attracted worried glances from his family members, he quickly added, "That was a joke. I would never beat up my prisoners. Not even the nasty ones."

"Nugent confessed to the whole thing," Chase chimed in. "Said he thought that if Ray and Toby were out of the picture Regan would come crying to him, and eventually develop feelings deeper than mere friendship. When that didn't happen, he decided she had to die."

"Yeah, a real Romeo, that one," said Alec.

"I think it's sad," intimated Marge, who was officiating the carving of a big slice of roast that she'd prepared on the grill just in case her husband's barbecue prowess failed them.

"Yeah, it's pretty sad," Odelia agreed. "But at least Regan is fine. And Jason Nugent will be punished for his crimes."

"I still don't get how you got it," Chase said, returning to one of his favorite themes. "I mean, those hunches of yours are quickly becoming the stuff of legend, Poole."

Odelia shrugged and took a sip of her wine, her eyes sparkling as much as the wine did. She wasn't going to reveal her big secret to Chase, who would never understand.

I cast a look at Vesta, who'd been remarkably quiet throughout the evening.

"What's the matter with Grandma?" asked Dooley, following my gaze. "She hasn't spoken a word all day. It's not like her to be in silence. And when she put out my bowl she gave me an extra cuddle and said, 'You're the only one in this house who truly loves me, Dooley. My one true friend. The only one who would never betray me.' What was that all about?"

We watched as Grandma Muffin sat cloaked in resolute silence, her lips pressed together in a thin line and her wrinkly face a thundercloud. She was even refusing to take nourishment, causing Marge to dart occasional exasperated glances in her direction.

"The thing is, Dooley, your human has been very naughty again."

Dooley uttered a groan. "What did she do this time?"

"Apparently when Tex and Marge gifted her an iPhone and a remarkably affordable cell phone plan so she could call her friends, she quickly discovered a fun game in the App Store."

"What kind of game?"

"Well, it's called 'Game of Phones.' The trick is to select as many world leaders as you can, and then call them for as long as possible. The person with the most world leaders on the leaderboard and the most phone time racked up wins a cruise to the Bahamas."

"So that's why she was calling Angela Merkel in the middle of the night!"

"I think she's hardly slept all week. She's been chatting non-stop with these non-existent world leaders all this time."

"Non-existent? You mean…"

I leveled a grim look at him. "Do you really think the German Chancellor would give a little old lady from Hampton Cove, USA, the time of day? Or listen to her rambling advice?"

"But Angela Merkel talked back to her. And so did this Ban Ki-moon and the others."

"Artificial intelligence automated response system," I said, repeating what Odelia had told me before dinner. "Grandma was talking to a bot, Dooley. Just a stupid computer bot."

"So what's so naughty about that? It must be fun to pretend-talk to the President."

"The thing is, Game of Phones is a scam. You pay an exorbitant amount of money for every minute you chat with their bots, and since Gran gave them Tex's credit card details…"

Dooley slapped a paw to his brow. "Oh, dear. Not again."

"Yes, again. So when Tex got his credit card bill this morning…"

"He wasn't happy."

"He was very unhappy. And then he confiscated Vesta's iPhone."

"And now she's unhappy."

"Come on, Mom," said Uncle Alec to his mother now. "You have to eat something. You'll starve to death!"

"So be it," croaked Grandma, her arms crossed defiantly over her chest. "This family hates me, so I hate them back." She wagged a bony finger. "If I die, it's on all of you!"

"You'll get your phone back once I figure out how to have it kid-proofed," said Tex.

She darted a look at him that no mother should ever

direct at her son-in-law. "For your information, I'm not a child, Tex!"

"As long as you act like one, you'll be treated as one," Tex said cheerfully. "Sausage, anyone?" He presented a plate with six blackened sausages. Uncle Alec, Odelia and Chase took one look at the incinerated carcasses and demurred, preferring Marge's roast instead.

"I want my phone," said Grandma mutinously. "You can't do this to me. This is a human rights violation and I'm gonna call Ban Ki-moon the minute I get my phone back."

"That wasn't the real Ban Ki-moon, Mom," said Marge gently. "That was just a computer bot in the Philippines pretending to be Ban Ki-moon so it could scam you."

"I don't care. He told me I could be the next Secretary-General of the United Nations. Said I had the gumption and the wherewithal to save the planet and restore world peace to a troubled humanity! Do you really think a fake Ban Ki-moon would say those things to me?"

"Look, Ban Ki-moon isn't even the Secretary-General anymore," Odelia pointed out, holding up her phone and displaying a Wikipedia page. "It's a guy called António Guterres."

"Don't you believe that stuff," said Gran stubbornly. "Everybody knows Wikipedia is fake news. I talked to Ban Ki-moon, and Angela Merkel, and Putin, and the President, and they all had nice things to say about me. Said I might get the Nobel Peace Prize for the work I do. And now that I finally get some recognition from some very important people, my own family turns against me!" She got up. "You know what? I don't need this crap. I'm leaving!"

They watched, jaws dropped, as she stalked off.

"Ma! Where are you going?" asked Uncle Alec.

"To Washington! Where I'm appreciated! I'm gonna talk

to the President in person. Last time we spoke he said he'd make me Secretary of State. I'm gonna remind him."

"Ma! Come back here!" Alec said, throwing down his napkin and chasing after her.

"Never! I'm destined for greatness! You can't hold me back!"

She disappeared around the corner of the house, still going strong, with Uncle Alec in hot pursuit. Their voices died away, and Dooley muttered, "Who's going to feed me now?"

"She'll be back," I told him. "She might be nuts, but she's not that nuts."

"How long before she'll come crawling back?" asked Odelia.

"I give her two hours," said Tex.

"One hour," said Marge. "She hasn't eaten, remember?"

"You've got one crazy family, Poole," said Chase with a grin. "And I like it!" he hastened to add when she quirked an eyebrow in his direction.

Yep. That's us. One crazy family. And as I watched Brutus and Harriet canoodling nearby, and Uncle Alec chase his mother around and around the house, and Chase press a kiss on Odelia's lips—and Tex doing the same with Marge—I thought about Dooley's words. When was I finally going to find love? I thought about Clarice, roaming her beloved woods again, and Charlie's Dieber Babes, one collection of fine but ultimately vapid cats, and then glanced at my buddy Dooley—my best friend and wingman—and sighed happily.

I had friends and family, I had food and my health. Why spoil it with romance?

A chicken wing rolled into my bowl, accompanied by a peck on the top of my head from Odelia, and I watched as she and Chase disappeared through the hedge, holding hands.

"What are they up to, you think?" asked Dooley.

"Nookie," I told him.

"What's a nookie, Max?" he asked.

"Um…"

"Is it like a cookie?"

"Yes. Yes, it is."

He smiled. "I love cookies."

In short order, Tex and Marge disappeared into the house, Brutus and Harriet disappeared into the bushes, and the backyard was suddenly empty.

"Are they all going for cookies?" asked Dooley.

"Yup. Everybody loves a cookie."

We sat in silence for a moment, watching as Uncle Alec and Grandma Muffin came around the corner of the house once more. Grandma appeared out of breath, for she plunked down in her chair, glanced around and, noticing the rest of the family had split, sliced off a piece of roast, dug her spoon into the bowl of potatoes, and started tucking in.

Uncle Alec, also dropping into a chair, watched her with a contented smile.

Silence reigned, only interrupted by Grandma's smacking noises.

"You know what, Max?" asked Dooley finally.

"What?"

"Chase is probably right. The Pooles are a little crazy, aren't they?"

"That, they definitely are."

"But I still love them."

"So do I, Dooley. So do I."

And then we followed Grandma's example and tucked in, too.

Life with the Pooles might not be perfect, but it was never boring.

# EXCERPT FROM PURRFECT PERIL (THE MYSTERIES OF MAX 7)

**Prologue**

Burt Goldsmith poured another bottle of bubbly over his head, the effervescent gold nectar fizzing as it hit his mane, trickled down his trim physique, and splashed across the floor of the shower cabin. He rubbed the expensive liquor into his remarkably well-preserved face—remarkable for a seventy-eight-year-old—and his thick thatch of white hair—another astonishing feat—and sighed contentedly. Other, lesser people might enjoy rubbing conditioner into their scalp but as the reigning Most Fascinating Man in the World he preferred a substance somewhat less mundane. A nice bottle of Chateauneuf du Pape served his purposes just fine. He would have preferred Piper-Heidsieck but the hotel he was currently gracing with his exclusive presence had run out of his favorite brand so the Chateauneuf would have to do.

And it did. As soon as he'd splashed the contents of a second bottle across the remainder of his corpus, he was ready to face another day. He stepped from the pink marble shower into the pink marble bathroom and strode confidently into the adjoining bedroom, not bothering with a towel, sprightly moving to the window overlooking Hampton Cove's busiest street. He didn't go so far as to step out onto the balcony to greet the milling throngs below, but he did fling the window wide and sampled a lungful of air, planting his feet wide, hands on his thighs. The Most Fascinating Man in the World didn't do towels. The Most Fascinating Man in the World air-dried.

As he stood there, his white hair flapping in the breeze like a lion's mane, he glanced to the side table that bookended the bed and noticed a silver salver with a single bottle of beer and a note. He remembered hearing the room service person announcing his arrival and shouting him in from the bathroom. He hadn't ordered room service, but figured another fan had left him another little present. His lady fans were always sending him personal items like edible panties or lacy little things accompanied by cheeky invitations to join them for lunch or dinner or—even more interestingly—into their boudoir.

The bottle of beer disappointed him. At first he presumed Tracy Sting had sent it up. A reminder of their lunch date. Tracy represented Dos Siglas, the well-known Mexican beer brand for whom Burt had made the popular Most Fascinating Man in the World commercials for the past fifteen years. He'd come to the Hamptons to shoot another commercial and Tracy was here to set everything up and make sure Burt had everything he needed and more. His idea of more, however, wasn't a bottle of Dos Siglas. Personally he despised the stuff. Dishwater, he liked to call it. After all, beer was the drink of the plebs. He preferred champagne, the nectar of the gods and godly men like Burt Goldsmith.

As he stood there, his hairy chest thrust out, he suddenly noticed there was something off about this particular bottle.

It didn't have the typical slender shape of Dos Siglas. Instead it was squat and plump, like a bottle of Tres Siglas, Dos Siglas's main competitor.

A sudden rage ripped through him. He knew who had sent him this bottle. Curt Pigott, the Most Compelling Man in the World. A man openly challenging his dominion as the world's premier interesting man at every turn. A man dying to steal his crown. He growled a few words unfit for print under his breath, his very short and very manly beard bristling with rage, his bronze physique shedding those final few drops of Chateauneuf du Pape, and balled his fists.

This was the third time this week Curt had done this. Taunting him. Challenging him. Trying to get under his skin.

It wouldn't work. Nothing got under the skin of the Most Fascinating Man in the World unless he sent it a personal monogrammed invitation to do so.

He crossed the floor to the side table in three powerful strides. He picked up the note, ascertaining that, yes, the bottle had indeed been sent by the Most Compelling Man in the World, and yes, it was a bottle of Tres Siglas prime ale. His dark eyes shooting sheets of flame, he crumpled up the note, picked up the bottle, which was cold to the touch, drops of condensation dappling the amber surface, and aimed it at the trashcan where it landed with a dull thud.

The explosion that blasted through the room took only milliseconds to turn the Most Fascinating Man in the World into the Most Fascinating Dead Man in the World, and Burt's nice hotel room into a conflagration of fire and fury.

**Chapter One**

Odelia Poole walked briskly along the street, her purse hiked high, her light blond hair bouncing jauntily around her shoulders, her slender frame clad in her usual work costume of white T, jeans and sneakers. She was on her way to one of the more exciting interviews of her career as a reporter for the Hampton Cove Gazette. Perhaps even the Most Exciting Interview in the World, she thought with a slight grin, as the interviewee she was about to meet was an actor who had made a name for himself as the Most Fascinating Man in the World, featuring in dozens of well-received ad campaigns for Dos Siglas beer.

Initially her editor Dan Goory had wanted to conduct the interview, big fan as he was of Burt Goldsmith and the man's body of work. But Odelia had insisted. She couldn't wait to meet the man—the legend—the icon. She had her list of questions written out, the recording app on her phone ready, and only a few more minutes separated her from the sit-down.

She glanced up at the Hampton Cove Star, the boutique hotel in downtown Hampton Cove, located right across the street from the Vickery General Store on Main Street, where all Hampton Covians like to stock up on supplies and shoot the breeze with Wilber Vickery, store owner and one of the town's mainstays and longtime citizens.

She waved a jolly hello to Wilber, who stood greeting the customers in front of his store, and was just about to enter the hotel when a familiar figure rounded the corner and gave her a happy smile. It was the bespectacled figure of Philippe Goldsmith, Burt's grandson and the person who'd set up the interview.

She halted in her tracks and returned the young man's smile. Philippe didn't look anything like his famous grandfather. He was in his mid-twenties, pale to the point of pasty, pudgy to the point of chubby, and nerdy to the point of *Big Bang's* Sheldon Cooper awkward. Philippe dragged a hand through his straggly dark hair, pushed his horn-rimmed spectacles up his bulbous nose, and gave her a hesitant smile. "Oh, hi, Miss Poole," he said.

"Hey, Philippe. Out shopping?"

He glanced down at the bulky bag he was carrying. "Oh, right. Yes. Yeah, just picking up some supplies for my granddad. The man enjoys his creature comforts." He pulled a carton box from the bag. Judging from the label it held a bottle of Piper-Heidsieck champagne. He held it up. "He uses this as conditioner if you can believe it."

She arched an eyebrow. "Conditioner?"

"Yeah, he says nothing tones and moisturizes the scalp like high-quality bubbly. In fact he credits champagne as the secret ingredient that has allowed him to keep his hair so luxuriant and shiny in spite of his advanced age." He clasped a hand in front of his mouth. "Oops. I probably shouldn't have said that. Especially to a reporter such as yourself."

She laughed. "The advanced age bit or the champagne secret?"

"Both," he said with an engaging grin. "Off the record?"

She nodded, tucking away these little tidbits for later use in her article.

"For a man who's about to enter his eighth decade he looks remarkably well."

"That's definitely true," she agreed. Though she'd wondered if it was Photoshop or Hollywood trickery that made Burt Goldsmith look so ageless. Apparently it wasn't.

"Anyway, we better go up," Philippe said. "Granddad doesn't like to be kept waiting."

"I'm ready if you are."

And Philippe had just opened his mouth to retort when there was an ear-splitting bang and something seemed to explode overhead. Odelia glanced up just in time to see flames shooting out from a second-floor window and a round object being catapulted down to the sidewalk. The round object came to a full stop against her foot, and as she looked down she saw that it was nothing other than the head of Burt Goldsmith himself.

The head was smoking, as if it had been on fire, and was still wearing that typical Most Fascinating Man in the World smirk, that roguish Sean Connery glint in those dark eyes, and a bemused expression on that handsomely bearded face. Burt Goldsmith's lips were parted, as if on the verge of delivering his famous line, 'Stay cool my friends.'

And as she stared down at the grotesque head in horror, she had to agree that Philippe was right: the man was remarkably well-preserved. Only now he was also very dead.

Next to her sounded a soft yelp, and the next moment Philippe had collapsed and was lying prostrate on the sidewalk, right next to the mortal remains of his famous granddad.

The Most Fascinating Grandson in the World had fainted.

**Chapter Two**

I awoke with a start, a powerful sense that something was awry hanging over me like a pall. I opened one eye then the other, and yawned cavernously. I stretched my limbs and glanced up at the bed. As a rule, I like to sleep at the foot of Odelia's bed, but ever since she bought herself one of those box spring contraptions I'm having a hard time navigating my approach shot. The thing is, you hit a box spring, and the box spring hits you right back. More than once I've landed on my tush on the floor, wondering what the hell happened.

How humans manage to land on the bed and stay there is a mystery to me.

I blinked against the invading light that peeped through the curtains and wondered once more what had awakened me. As far as I knew Odelia was still sound asleep, as she should be. I'm her official wake-up call, after all, and since I'd just woken up myself, it stood to reason my human was still in bed.

So why this sense that something was wrong? And then it hit me. The music. Odelia likes to wake up to the tunes of light pop music. Rihanna or Dua Lipa or Ariana Grande. At the moment some cowboy was crooning about being kicked in the gut by the woman he loved and lost. That didn't sound like Odelia. That sounded more like…

An awful sense of foreboding jarred my teeth like a kick to the butt.

Oh, no.

Not again.

I took the leap and landed on the bed. And what I saw there turned my blood to ice.

Chase.

Chase Kingsley.

The burly cop was lying in Odelia's bed. His long, curly brown hair draped across Odelia's pillow. His muscular body covered by Odelia's comforter. His handsome face buried in Odelia's Betty Boop pajama top.

I stared at the cop.

Suddenly, he opened one eye and stared back at me!

Man stared at cat.

Cat stared at man.

It was a moment fraught with extreme emotion, not to mention tension.

Then he yawned and stretched and slapped the empty space next to him.

He frowned in confusion. "You have any idea where…" He glanced at me and smiled a wry smile. "Why am I talking to a damn cat? Of course you don't know where Odelia is.

And even if you did, you wouldn't be able to tell me, would you, little buddy?"

He patted me roughly on the head—more a prod than a pat—and swung his feet to the floor. As usual, he was dressed in nothing but a tank top and a pair of boxers, his brawny arms all biceps and triceps and who-knows-what-else-ceps. Chase Kingsley's body is all muscular bumps in all kinds of places and the kind of washboard stomach human females go all goo-goo-ga-ga over, drooling at the mouth, their spine and knees turning to jelly.

You see, Chase is my human's boyfriend, and apparently boyfriends are supposed to sleep in the beds of their girlfriends. No idea why, though according to Harriet, the cat who lives next door with Odelia's mom and dad, it might have something to do with babies.

No idea what, exactly, but I have a sneaking suspicion I'm going to find out in the near future if this keeps up. Chase has been 'sleeping over' four nights in a row now, and judging from Odelia's furtive glances in my direction, the cop just might become a fixture.

I don't mind admitting I don't like it. I like things the way they were: just me, Odelia, and my best buddy Dooley, who also lives next door. The three of us, happy as clams.

And now this, this, this... intruder!

Blake Shelton was still wailing away in the background—he's Chase's favorite warbler. The former Sexiest Man Alive is the Hunkiest Man Alive's favorite singer. Of course he is.

Chase threw the curtains wide and sunlight streamed into the room. Then he disappeared into the bathroom and moments later the shower turned on and steam started pouring into the bedroom.

I heaved a ragged sigh and directed a nasty look at Chase's phone, where Mr. Shelton was now gibbering on and on about a hillbilly bone, whatever that was. From pure frustration my skin broke out in hives and I raised my hind paw to scratch that itch.

Suddenly, and without warning, another itch broke out, this time behind my left ear, and I raised my hind paw a little higher to address that itch, too. It was no use, though, as seemingly all across my voluminous body my skin erupted in an annoying cascade of itches and for the next five minutes, while Mr. Hunk's voice burst into song in the bathroom next door, I busied myself fighting a regular forest fire of itchiness all over my feline bod.

"Max!" suddenly a voice called out from the door.

I glanced over. It was Dooley, my best friend and wingman. Whereas I am of big-boned stock, with blorange fur, Dooley is a gray ragamuffin and considerably slighter. At the moment he was looking troubled. Now the thing you need to know about Dooley is that he always looks troubled. He is what you would call a worrier. But right now he was looking even more worried and troubled than usual.

"I know," I said. "I don't like it either."

"It's terrible!" he cried. "How long has this been going on?"

"Weeks. Months. I don't know. One day everything is fine, and then suddenly. Boom. Your life is turned upside down. It's not fair is what it is. Not fair to spring this on us."

"You've had it for months?" he asked, joining me on the bed. For some strange reason the box spring only kicks back when I try to land on it. Dooley, on the other hand, landed gracefully on all fours and gave me a look of concern. "You should have told me."

"I did tell you. I've been telling you all the time. I've done nothing *but* tell you."

"Where is it?" he asked, glancing down at the itch I was currently trying to remedy.

I gestured with my tail to the bathroom. "In there."

He glanced over, a puzzled look on his furry face. "Huh?"

"He's in there! God's gift to women is taking a shower, acting as if he owns the place, can you believe it? I swear to Sheba, Dooley, that man is moving in."

Dooley blinked. "You were talking about Chase?"

"Weren't you?"

In response, he raised his hind paw and started scratching furiously behind his right ear. "No. I. Was. Not," he said between grunts and scratches. The itch finally abated and he added, panting slightly, "I was talking about these terrible itches. These horrible, annoying itches. They started up last night and I can't seem to get rid of them."

"Itches? You have itches?"

"I have—and so do you. And so, for that matter, do Brutus and Harriet."

"That's not good."

"It's bad, Max," he said, his whiskers puckering up into an expression of extreme concern. "Do you think we caught some kind of disease? Do you think…" He swallowed visibly and lowered his voice to a whisper. "Do you think… we're going to… die?"

I groaned. "We're not going to die, Dooley. It's just an itch. It will pass."

He flapped his paws a bit. "But we all have them, Max!" His eyes widened to the size of saucers. "It's a virus! A virus that will wipe out the entire feline population!"

We'd watched a movie called *Contagion* the other night with Odelia and Chase. It was about Gwyneth Paltrow who shakes hands with a chef in Hong Kong and dies and pretty soon everyone else also dies except for her husband Matt Damon who doesn't die. It was horrible. I kept my paws in front of my eyes the entire time. Can you imagine even Kate Winslet died? After surviving that whole Titanic thing she goes and dies from some silly little virus. And now every time someone coughs Dooley thinks they are going to die, too.

"But Brutus and Harriet have it, too, and I'll bet soon every cat in Hampton Cove will have it, and then it will spread to New York and the country and the world!" He gave a hiccup and grabbed my paw, which hurt, as he neglected to retract his claws. "We're all gonna die!"

Just in that moment Chase walked in from the bathroom and we both looked up. He had a towel strapped around his private parts and was toweling his long hair. He reminded me of that movie *Tarzan* we'd seen with that vampire from *True Blood*. I know, we watch a lot of television in this house. And you thought cats didn't watch TV. Huh. Think again.

"Oh, hey, Dooley," said Chase, spotting my friend sitting next to me. Then he grinned and shook his head. "I'm doing it again. Talking to a bunch of cats. I must be going loco."

Like a pair of synchronized swimmers, both Dooley and I raised our hind paws and started scratching ourselves behind the left ears, then the right ears, then under the chin.

Chase stopped rubbing his scalp with the towel and gave us a look of concern.

"Well, what do we have here?" he muttered.

He sat down on the bed, and for some reason began inspecting me, checking my fur here and there, carefully parting my blorange hair to look at that nice pink skin underneath. Then he subjected Dooley to the same procedure. Finally, he sat back, and glanced at a smattering of red spots on his ankle and nodded knowingly. "Well, I'll be damned."

Suddenly something jumped from my neck onto the bed. Something small and black.

Quick as lightning, Chase caught it between his fingernails, and studied it for a moment, before mashing it to bits, his face taking on a serious expression. He then gave me and

Dooley a long look of concern, not unlike a father about to give his daughter The Talk.

Oh, yes. I've seen movies where fathers give their daughters The Talk. But Chase wasn't my father, and I'm not his daughter, so why would he give me The Talk?

I braced myself for the worst, and judging from Dooley's claws digging into my skin, so did he.

"I hate to be the one to tell you this." Chase spoke earnestly and with surprising tenderness lacing his rumbling baritone. "But you guys got fleas."

Dooley and I shared a look of confusion. "Fleas?" I asked. "What are fleas?"

Dooley was quaking where he sat. "It's the virus! It's what killed Rose from Titanic!"

"Now, this is nothing to be concerned about," Chase continued gently, almost as if he could actually understand what Dooley was saying. "I'll tell Odelia and she'll take care of this straightaway." He patted my head again—another one of those awkward prods—and smiled. "What doesn't kill you makes you stronger. And fleas have never killed anyone. I think."

Dooley, who was on the verge of a full-scale panic attack, wailed, "We won't die?"

"Didn't you listen to the man?" I asked. "Fleas are going to make us stronger."

Another itch suddenly plagued me, and I reached with my hind paw to remedy it. But Chase beat me to the punch. He dove right in, and soon was extracting another one of those jumpy little bugs from my skin, mashing it to pieces between his fingernails.

Both Dooley and I stared at the guy like a pair of hobbits staring at Gandalf the Wizard. "He saved you, Max," said Dooley reverently. "He killed the killer bug."

"It's not a killer bug, Dooley," I said.

"He killed the killer bug with his bare hands."

"I'm telling you it's not a killer bug."

"He saved you. Chase saved you from the killer bug. He's a hero."

"It's not a killer bug and Chase is not a hero!"

But I had to admit that maybe—just maybe—I'd misjudged Odelia's boyfriend.

The man *was* a genuine hero. The fiercest fleaslayer the world had ever known.

**Chapter Three**

Back at the hotel Odelia was prepared for the worst when she followed her uncle up to the second floor of the Hampton Cove Star. Downstairs, the secondary crime scene had been sealed off from prying eyes by a screen, and techies from the Suffolk County Medical Examiner's office were busily scratching their heads as they stared down at Burt's head.

Upstairs, the hotel manager, an obsequious little man with a clean-shaven face and shifty eyes, led the way to the room where the tragedy had taken place. Odelia's uncle Alec Lip, Hampton Cove's chief of police, hiked up his gun belt, while Odelia and a few more boys and girls in blue followed in the big man's wake.

As the town's prime crime reporter—or quite frankly the town's only reporter, prime, crime or otherwise—Odelia had a front-row seat to most investigations her uncle was involved in, as long as she was discreet and didn't print stuff in her paper that could hamper the investigation. A fine sleuth in her own right, she'd solved more than one crime in her time, a fact for which her uncle was more than appreciative.

"Where is Chase?" she asked now.

Her uncle cocked an eyebrow in her direction. "I should probably ask *you* that."

She blushed slightly. Chase had been living with Uncle Alec, but had been staying over at her place more and more frequently these past few weeks. She didn't know whether this was a good thing or a bad thing, but she had to admit she'd grown very fond of the cop.

"I called him," she said. "He said he'd be here."

Uncle Alec shrugged. "If he says he'll be here, he'll be here."

She glanced back at the line of cops following in her wake. They all looked away, but judging from their barely concealed smiles and pricked-up ears, they were eagerly listening in on the conversation. The whole station knew about her and Chase, and followed the budding romance with the kind of fervor usually reserved for the big Hollywood love stories.

The manager came to a full stop in front of an unremarkable door and inserted an unremarkable badge into the unremarkable slot. The mechanism gave a beep, then the door unceremoniously dropped out of its hinges and collapsed to the side, offering the stunned viewers a glance at the devastated room behind it. The place looked like a war zone.

"Oh, Lord," said the little manager, clasping his hands to his face. "Oh, dear. Oh, my."

"Not much left," said Uncle Alec gruffly, and ventured inside.

Odelia's uncle was a big man with a big belly and a big, round ruddy face. At last count he possessed three chins, two man boobs and two russet sideburns. The moment he stepped across the threshold, there was a loud creaking sound and something gave way.

One moment Uncle Alec was there—the next he was gone.

"Uncle!" Odelia cried, and took a step forward, only to be held back by the manager.

"Careful, Miss Poole, please," the man said in a breathless whisper.

They both glanced down into the chief-of-police-shaped hole at their feet. One floor down, Uncle Alec was staring up at them, looking slightly dazed and covered with chalk and debris. He was lying on a bed, which had broken his fall, an elderly lady lying next to him, clutching a sheet to her chest, and staring at him with a mixture of curiosity and surprise.

"I'm fine!" Alec called out to them, lifting an arm to indicate he was still alive. "The bed broke my fall."

Suddenly, the woman next to him said, "And my husband."

"Mh?" Alec asked.

The woman pointed to an object underneath Alec. "My husband broke your fall."

A muffled sound came from beneath the large man. "Kindly get off me, sir!"

Uncle Alec rolled from the bed, and a rumpled elderly gentleman appeared, his glasses askew. He took a few deep breaths, and proceeded to give the police chief his best scowl. "This is an outrage, sir. An outrage."

"I'm sorry," said the policeman. "And thank you."

The man was shaking his fist at the hotel manager now, visible through the hole in the ceiling. "I'm calling my travel agent, sir. This is not the kind of service I expected from this establishment! First that loud bang that woke us up and now this. Color me dissatisfied."

"You tell 'em, Earl," said his wife, still clutching the sheet to protect her modesty.

"I'm truly sorry, Mr. Assenheimer," the manager called out. "We'll comp you your room and your meals. And you can add a week to your stay. No expense."

"That's the least you can do," said the old man, slightly mollified.

Odelia stepped across the hole in the floor and carefully ventured into the room. The devastation was incredible. Walls, floor and ceiling blackened. The bed smashed against the wall. The windows blown out. In fact it was a miracle the damage had been contained to this one room. As far as she could determine—and she was no expert—the explosion must have taken place near the window, the brunt of the force directed outward.

"Maybe we should wait for the fire department, Miss Poole," said the manager.

She nodded, glancing around. Then her eyes landed on the remains of the man she'd come here to interview. His blackened and charred corpse—now conspicuously headless—had been flung onto the balcony and was now lying there, almost as if in leisurely repose. If she hadn't known better, she would have thought he was sunbathing. And had overdone it.

She narrowed her eyes. Was the man buck naked? It would appear so.

"Better step back, Odelia," her uncle's voice sounded from the door. He was scratching his chalky scalp. "This is something for the experts. Not much we can do here."

He was right, of course. There was absolutely nothing they could do here.

She directed a final look at Burt Goldsmith and shook her head. Such a tragic loss. The man might not have been in the prime of his life, but he still had so much to offer.

She stepped back into the corridor and the manager heaved an audible sigh of relief. He obviously did not want more people to crash through the floor and onto other guests.

Only now did she notice that up and down the corridor

doors had been opened and other hotel guests had appeared, discussing the recent events and anxiously awaiting further developments, like people do. And to her surprise she recognized several of the men who stood staring back at her. There was the Curt Pigott, Most Compelling Man in the World and the man who'd put Tres Siglas beer on the map, Bobbie Hawe, Most Attractive Man in the World and face of the Quattro Siglas brew, Jasper Hanson, Most Intriguing Man in the World, representing Cinco Siglas, Nestor Greco, Most Iconic Man in the World and iconic Seis Siglas figurehead, and even Dale Parson, who'd recently been voted Sexiest Man Alive.

What was this? A convention of the Most Interesting Men in the World?

Chief Alec's people spread out and started taking down information and asking these men what they'd seen or heard. They would do the same with the other hotel guests and staff, and hopefully learn what had happened in those crucial final moments of Burt's life.

ALSO BY NIC SAINT

**The Mysteries of Max**
Purrfect Murder
Purrfectly Deadly
Purrfect Revenge
Box Set 1 (Books 1-3)
Purrfect Heat
Purrfect Crime
Purrfect Rivalry
Box Set 2 (Books 4-6)
Purrfect Peril
Purrfect Secret
Purrfect Alibi
Box Set 3 (Books 7-9)
Purrfect Obsession
Purrfect Betrayal
Purrfectly Clueless
Box Set 4 (Books 10-12)
Purrfectly Royal
Purrfect Cut
Purrfect Trap
Purrfectly Hidden
Purrfect Kill

Purrfect Santa
Purrfectly Flealess

### Nora Steel
Murder Retreat

### The Kellys
Murder Motel

Death in Suburbia

### Emily Stone
Murder at the Art Class

### Washington & Jefferson
First Shot

### Alice Whitehouse
Spooky Times

Spooky Trills

Spooky End

Spooky Spells

### Ghosts of London
Between a Ghost and a Spooky Place

Public Ghost Number One

Ghost Save the Queen

Box Set 1 (Books 1-3)

A Tale of Two Harrys

Ghost of Girlband Past

Ghostlier Things

### Charleneland
Deadly Ride

Final Ride

**Neighborhood Witch Committee**

Witchy Start

Witchy Worries

Witchy Wishes

**Saffron Diffley**

Crime and Retribution

Vice and Verdict

Felonies and Penalties (Saffron Diffley Short 1)

**The B-Team**

Once Upon a Spy

**Tate-à-Tate**

Enemy of the Tates

**Ghosts vs. Spies**

The Ghost Who Came in from the Cold

**Witchy Fingers**

Witchy Trouble

Witchy Hexations

Witchy Possessions

Witchy Riches

Box Set 1 (Books 1-4)

**The Mysteries of Bell & Whitehouse**

One Spoonful of Trouble

Two Scoops of Murder

Three Shots of Disaster

Box Set 1 (Books 1-3)

A Twist of Wraith

A Touch of Ghost

A Clash of Spooks

Box Set 2 (Books 4-6)

The Stuffing of Nightmares

A Breath of Dead Air

An Act of Hodd

Box Set 3 (Books 7-9)

A Game of Dons

**Standalone Novels**

When in Bruges

The Whiskered Spy

**ThrillFix**

Homejacking

The Eighth Billionaire

The Wrong Woman

## ABOUT NIC

Nic Saint is the pen name for writing couple Nick and Nicole Saint. They've penned 70+ novels in the romance, cat sleuth, middle grade, suspense, comedy and cozy mystery genres. Nicole has a background in accounting and Nick in political science and before being struck by the writing bug the Saints worked odd jobs around the world (including massage therapist in Mexico, gardener in Italy, restaurant manager in India, and Berlitz teacher in Belgium).

When they're not writing they enjoy Christmas-themed Hallmark movies (whether it's Christmas or not), all manner of pastry, comic books, a daily dose of yoga (to limber up those limbs), and spoiling their big red tomcat Tommy.

Sign up for the no-spam newsletter and be the first to know when a new book comes out: nicsaint.com/newsletter.

www.nicsaint.com

- facebook.com/nicsaintauthor
- twitter.com/nicsaintauthor
- bookbub.com/authors/nic-saint
- amazon.com/author/nicsaint

Printed in Great Britain
by Amazon